JUST OUR LUCK

ALSO BY JULIA WALTON

Words on Bathroom Walls

JUST OUR LUCK

Julia Walton

Random House New York

Text copyright © 2020 by Julia Walton
Jacket art copyright © 2020 by Philip Pascuzzo

All rights reserved. Published in the United States by Random House Children's Books, a division of Penguin Random House LLC, New York.

Random House and the colophon are registered trademarks of Penguin Random House LLC.

Visit us on the Web! GetUnderlined.com

Educators and librarians, for a variety of teaching tools, visit us at RHTeachersLibrarians.com

Library of Congress Cataloging-in-Publication Data
Name: Walton, Julia, author.
Title: Just our luck / Julia Walton.
Description: First edition. | New York: Random House, [2020]
Summary: "Leo has always been told to stay away from Evey Paros, but after his anxiety disorder causes a fight at school, he has no choice but to ask for her help" —Provided by publisher.
Identifiers: LCCN 2019036252 (print) | LCCN 2019036253 (ebook) |
ISBN 978-0-399-55092-8 (hardcover) | ISBN 978-0-399-55093-5 (library binding) |
ISBN 978-0-399-55094-2 (ebook)
Subjects: CYAC: Anxiety disorders—Fiction. | High schools—Fiction. | Schools—Fiction. |
Greek Americans—Fiction.
Classification: LCC PZ7.1.W3642 Ju 2020 (print) | LCC PZ7.1.W3642 (ebook) |
DDC [Fic]—dc23

The text of this book is set in 12-point Bembo.
Interior design by Trish Parcell

Printed in the United States of America
10 9 8 7 6 5 4 3 2 1
First Edition

For Kiria Isa,

who told me all the stories

I wasn't supposed to hear

1

I didn't lie. Not really.

I just didn't provide all the details.

Yia Yia would have said that's lying too because you can feel it in your stomach when you're holding something back.

Not holding back was the problem, though, because I lunged at him first. I just didn't tell anybody that.

And I should have known better. It was rule number one of the two rules that Yia Yia drilled into my head before she died.

Rule Number 1: "Bad luck follows lies, agapi mou."

Rule Number 2: "Leave the Paros family alone."

Yes, he hit me. But that's not the full story, and it *would* be lying to say that it wasn't just a little bit my fault.

The thing with anxiety is that people think it makes you run from a fight, but that's not always true. At least not for me. Sometimes it makes you defensive.

What happens for me is that when that hot, panicky feeling rises up, I just need to get it out of my system, and sometimes the easiest way to do that is to be a jerk. Lash out as quickly as possible to get that instant relief of setting the bad thing free. Just as long as it leaves me alone—as long as it's not gnawing on the hardware in my brain—I'm cool.

Anyway, it's actually the school's fault this happened. Service hours are required, and I've always signed up for the jobs that are mostly solitary, like reshelving library books. But this time they assigned us jobs, and someone thought it would be a good idea for me to sell candy at the Snack Shack.

It was the first day back from winter break, so of course the place was swarming with people holding their sweaty money from the holidays, trying to elbow their way to the cash register. And I was behind the counter, responsible for giving them the sugar to keep this orgy of energy going. Jesus Christ. What had I done to deserve this?

I kept telling myself it was only for today, but as more people filled the room, I started to hear a loud buzzing in my ears.

All the Sour Patch Kids went first. Then the fresh cookies. Then the Starbursts.

One guy, Jordan Swansea, gave me forty dollars for three big containers of Red Vines and told me to keep the change as he walked out and distributed them in handfuls to the rest of his impossibly tall group of jock friends.

Overpaying for Red Vines in the Snack Shack just so you can drop money on the counter in front of everyone and walk away is a classic symbol of douchebaggery. That's probably unfair, but he has that kind of vibe. Maybe it's not such a big deal for rich people. I wouldn't know. My high school sits in the middle of a lot of wealthy neighborhoods, so even though my family has always been solidly middle-class, that almost translates to poor here.

That's what I was thinking when Drake Gibbons, the second douchebag of the day, got to the front of the line. As I was counting back change, he interrupted me. I should probably note that he does that a lot. Interrupts, I mean. He's been in my class since his family moved here in third grade, and he has always been annoying. He doesn't really have a filter, which means he was usually responsible for the truest (and meanest) nicknames doled out in elementary school.

I was doing fine trying to ignore the noise and the people, but instead of waiting for me to finish, Drake grabbed a Clif Bar, dropped a wrinkled twenty into the cash box, and said, "Nineteen, dude."

I would have pegged him for a Slim Jim kinda guy.

"Just a sec." I was still helping this girl who was trying to pick out all the green apple Jolly Ranchers from the plastic box in front of her, but Drake didn't want to wait for his change.

"Here, dude, let me help you with that." He tried to reach into my cash box, but I pulled it back.

"Just a sec. I'm not done with that."

Jolly Rancher Girl, who also went by Cassie and was in my algebra class, was taking her sweet-ass time pulling out her candy, and I was trying to move her along while Drake kept putting his hand over the counter to grab his change. It wasn't clicking for him that I was still helping someone else. Like he heard me but didn't hear me. If that makes any sense.

"Dude, I'll help you. It's nineteen bucks." He was still leaning over the counter. Still in my space. Close enough for me to smell the protein shake on his breath. Cassie glared at him, but he ignored her too.

"Just wait," I said, gritting my teeth. I put up my hand. The noise in the room was giving me a stomachache, and I had to start over counting back change for the second time.

Then Drake stage-whispered, "Uh-oh, better not make Fat Leo mad."

I glared at him. Fat Leo was the best nickname he could give me as a kid. Since I subsisted on a diet of moussaka and souvlaki and my pudgy belly stretched most of my clothes, Fat Leo was a suitable choice, I guess, but completely without vision.

He swiped for the cash box, and Cassie once again tried to get me to finish her transaction. That's when the crowd turned ugly.

"Some of us are HANGRY. Just give me my Funyuns, dude!" said a guy at the back.

"And breath mints," said his girlfriend.

A bunch of people laughed, but a few other people started sounding really annoyed about the holdup.

The laughter rumbled in my head, making it feel like my temples had a heartbeat.

Why am I here around people and not hiding in a dark corner? Why isn't that a service hours option?

There was another grab for the cash box, and as I yanked it out of Drake's reach, I could see people watching with curiosity.

"Jesus," said Drake. "Just let me grab my change."

The sound reverberated in my head like a microphone screeching with audio feedback.

"Dude, you got a fifty-seven on your last math test. You think I trust you to figure out your own change?"

I could see immediately that it was embarrassing to him. I handed Cassie her change and then counted out his nineteen bucks, slowly. Deliberately. Then someone pushed him out of the way and I didn't see him until later that afternoon.

I had a study period before gym. Instead of wandering to the library as usual, I found one of three spots normally unoccupied by people, in a hall just outside the computer lab.

I pulled out some blue chenille yarn and started crocheting a mati.

The mati was the first thing I'd ever learned to make. It's

a black circle in a blue circle surrounded by a white circle. An eye that Greeks put up to keep the devil away. To ward off bad luck. I was going to leave this one at Yia Yia's grave. I put all my focus into making small, even stitches, even though I totally heard Drake when he walked up to me.

I ignore people when I'm focused. Especially since my mind was still running from the Snack Shack incident. In the grand scheme of things, it's just one guy being kind of a dick. But anxiety, remember? Sometimes small stuff hits big.

"Hey, man, that was kinda messed up what you did today."

I didn't even look up. Didn't even try to acknowledge him. Until he pulled my yarn out of my hands.

That's when I lost it.

I didn't hit him, but I did lunge forward and swipe for my yarn, which he was holding near his face, and since it probably looked like I was going to hit him, he hit me first. In the face.

In movies they make it look so easy for the hero to get beaten to a gross, bloody pulp and then instantly get back to fighting, but they underestimate pain. Or maybe it's just that my soft, squishy body could not deal with the slow-motion bulldozing from Drake's fist.

He is way faster and bigger and stronger. He probably didn't know what to do when he actually knocked me down. But he *did* run for the nurse. And even before I hit the ground, I knew my lip would be a meaty disaster. I can only hope the blood that pooled around my body scarred him for life. But then I passed out.

Being unconscious at the time, I can't really know for sure.

The janitor was the first person I saw when I woke up. I heard him mutter something about the mess he had to clean up.

Nice.

There were no other witnesses. It was just me and my rap sheet of other incidents that labeled me as a problem, even though all those other incidents were bad stuff happening TO me.

Guess they read that as bad stuff happening BECAUSE of me.

Because I mostly just want to be left alone, and for some reason that makes other guys with nothing better to do go, *Let's piss on his backpack and see if he notices.*

The best part was when the principal called my dad in to talk. It wasn't my first time being called in to the principal, but it was the first time in high school. And since I'm a junior now, I'm a little surprised it took this long.

Middle school was another story, though. It had been a shitstorm of counselor visits and principal interventions that never seemed to end because people (i.e., other kids) always want to get a reaction from the Quiet Kid, even when the Quiet Kid isn't bothering anyone.

I couldn't hear the beginning of the conversation through the door, but eventually I knew it wasn't going well when Dad started muttering loudly.

In Greek.

Translated, this is what he said: "What he needs is to stop acting so sensitive and misunderstood. He needs to learn how to deal with people. Or at the very least, how to defend himself."

"Why did this happen?" Dad finally said in English.

And the next part I heard clear as a bell. So did everyone else in the administration office, because the principal had been trying, without success, to speak over my dad's muttering, and he forgot to use his inside voice.

"Leo doesn't get along with his peers!"

The secretary behind the counter jumped a little, then looked over at me and pretended nothing had happened. I had to guess all the other things the principal was probably telling my dad that he already knew, though, because he lowered his voice again.

Things like:

Leo doesn't play well with others.

Leo doesn't participate in any school activities.

Leo keeps to himself.

Leo struggles with group assignments and presentations.

Leo knits a lot.

That last one is when my dad would have died of shame. Even though Yia Yia was *his* mom. She taught me to knit. She basically taught me how to do anything and everything with yarn and most fibers, and he will never forgive her for it, because it's not something men do. Well, it's not something they're supposed to do.

"This might help you relax, agapi mou," Yia Yia said.

It is relaxing, but I probably shouldn't have been doing it at school.

I shouldn't do anything that draws attention. I shouldn't do anything I have to explain, because then I invite people in. It's like asking them to comment on something I enjoy.

Like a guy riding a unicycle down the street. Maybe leave him the fuck alone.

Ride your weird one-wheeled human conveyance machine, dude.

Anyway, that's what happened.

I got into a fight with Drake, and my dad had to come get me from school. He drove me home with a tissue shoved up my nose, and neither of us spoke the entire ride, which wasn't unusual, since we don't speak much anyway.

But there was a moment when the principal asked me what happened and I didn't say anything about how I'd swiped at Drake first. I didn't say that it had been a preemptive strike.

I just said: "He hit me."

Which, like I said, wasn't a lie, but it wasn't really the whole truth either. And you can always feel those kinds of lies when they sneak out. Like they're hiding under your tongue, just waiting for the opportunity to escape.

Now I have to meet with Drake in the guidance counselor's office to work through our differences, because even though Drake punched me, the principal was clearly concerned about my knitter/loner/quiet-kid label and wanted someone to keep an eye on me.

So, yeah, Drake was a douchebag, but maybe I could

have handled it differently, maybe, if I hadn't gotten so defensive.

Maybe I wouldn't have said that.

Maybe I could've been nicer.

Fuck. How did this happen?

2

Dear Journal,

Jesus, I'm writing in a journal. One step up from talking to myself. I can't believe this is my life now. I can't believe this is what happens after a fight.

Generally a fight will get you detention. And maybe a black eye if you're lucky.

It doesn't trap you in a room full of people who start every class by thanking everyone for showing up to "share our energy on this magnificent journey."

Because now I'm here in this yoga class where I am forced to keep this journal to track my progress.

But wait. It's not just yoga. It is HOT yoga.

Really absurdly HOT yoga that, miraculously, has not

yet turned my body into beef jerky despite the fact that I am completely drained of all liquid because it has seeped out of my body.

My eyebrows are filled with sweat, and my underwear has become a bucket for the slip-and-slide that is my butt crack.

This is a series of events I was not prepared for.

But how did I get here?

Oh yeah.

Because after the fight, my dad decided I needed to learn to defend myself.

It's his most recent attempt to make me a man. Like an actual man. Not a shrimpy, artsy, knitting elf child who dabbles in photography.

He didn't actually call me those things, but he has this look he gives me, and believe me, that's what the look says.

But he *is* the one who uses the word *dabbles* when he talks about my photography, because he doesn't want me or anyone else to confuse it with something that makes money. Or something that matters.

Guess it only mattered when Mom did it.

Photography. Cameras. That was Mom. The only memory I have that's real and not based on a story from Yia Yia is one of me holding Mom's camera and her teaching me how to shoot.

Her pictures were a way for me to remember stuff. To remember her.

Dad is right to some extent, I guess. I've never taken a

photography class. Everything I know about cameras and taking pictures is from books I've read at the library and documentaries I've watched on Netflix. All of my technique and everything I've learned about exposure, angles, color, lighting, etc.—it's mostly stuff I've had to mess up and figure out on my own.

But when I look through a lens, I know exactly the kind of photo I want to take. I know what needs to be captured. I know how to make the camera do what I want.

Yia Yia encouraged me, but none of that matters to Dad. The photography and the knitting are embarrassing to him, which became even more obvious when last night he enrolled me in a self-defense course. Not even a normal self-defense class that teaches you how to flip a guy if he comes up behind you. A hard-core teach-your-students-how-to-bite-off-a-chunk-of-their-assailant's-neck course taught by some guy named Brad Hardwick, because of course that's his name.

Dad said, "Leo, I'll be waiting in the car. Go to class. I'll be out here when you're done." Then he used the full force of his eyeballs. His eyeballs always protrude a little bit when he's mad.

That's how I learned what the word *protrude* means, when I was little. Because I needed to explain what my dad's eyeballs did when he was angry. They bulge. They swell. They look cartoony. He thinks the more he shoves his eyeballs out of their sockets, the easier it'll be for other people to take him seriously.

After ordering me inside and using the eyeballs, he turned on classical music like a serial killer and leaned back in his seat with a newspaper. An actual newspaper because he still refuses to read the news on his phone.

I had no choice but to get out of the car. I walked into the gigantic, sterilely clean lobby of the gym and stood in front of the glass window, watching two guys throw practice punches at each other for exactly fifteen seconds before I realized I was never going in that classroom. Ever.

But my options were limited. I couldn't go back out to my dad; he'd walk me into class himself. And I couldn't just stand in the lobby, because my dad could see me through the glass door from the car. So I walked up to the front desk, ready to confess my shame, and figured I would be honest.

"Look," I said to the girl behind the counter. "My dad enrolled me in that military self-defense class." I nodded toward the guys who were now beating the shit out of a weird plastic dummy. "But I need to take ANY CLASS BUT THAT."

And I wish I had noticed who she was before I started talking.

The girl was leaning on a stack of magazines and wearing a midnight-blue exercise headband over shiny dark brown hair. When she lifted her black eyes to meet mine, I realized exactly who she was. Yia Yia's voice came floating out from the great beyond with the only other rule she'd ever laid down: *Leave the Paros family alone.*

And yet here she was, Evey Paros. The youngest daughter of Costa and Maria Paros.

And for half a second, I wondered if she'd been told the same story I'd been told my whole life. If she had any idea that her family had cursed mine.

I felt like an idiot for thinking this.

Of course she didn't know about the curse. Of course she didn't believe in that crap.

I shook the thought off like I was afraid she might see it as a thought bubble above my head.

She pointed toward another room and said, "This class meets at the same time every day. It's Hot Yoga Teacher Training. We just had someone drop out. You can switch and nobody has to know." She whispered, "I won't tell a soul."

The room was filled with steam that was creeping out the door like mist in a horror movie. And the heat was already threatening to suffocate me, reaching out into the hall. It was like the portal to hell.

"Are you in?" Evey asked. She leaned forward, and it was difficult to focus because despite the obvious awkwardness of the situation and my promise to avoid her family, I couldn't look directly at her. And it wasn't *just* because she was beautiful, even though she was. God, she was. She had this look like she'd just risen out of the sea with her dark hair flung wildly over her shoulder, dragging the corpses of her enemies behind her. A perfect combination of beautiful and scary.

So yeah, it was more her confidence than anything else.

I turned back to the fight class, where all the guys had started chanting, and noticed Drake had just walked in as well.

WTF.

It would be kinda awkward for me to take a class to defend myself against someone else currently taking the same fucking class, no?

The chanting got louder.

WE ARE WARRIORS.

WE ARE WARRIORS.

WARRRRRRRIOOOOOOOORS!

So yeah, I was in.

Because, holy shit, what choice did I have?

But then Evey gave me a look that made my Yia Yia's warnings about Greek women seem like logical, real-world advice.

She entered a few things into her computer to transfer me from one class to another, then said innocently, "All done. There you go."

It seemed so simple. I said "Thanks" and moved awkwardly toward the festering swamp that was the yoga room.

But then she called out, "For the record, I don't believe in curses, but you do owe me now. I bet we can work something out for the class switch."

I skidded to a stop and swung back around to stare at her, thinking maybe she was kidding. There was no way she'd actually just said that. The curse was something my Yia Yia just made up, right?

Then her black eyes darkened, and I swear the room

got colder as she inclined her head toward the parking lot, where my dad was sitting in his car. She put her finger to her lips and whispered, "Shhhhh."

Evey's eyes are hypnotic.

She looks at you, and you wonder briefly if you've disappointed her somehow and if the last thing you said was so unbelievably stupid that you can never retract it.

And there was Yia Yia's voice again.

Leave the Paros family alone.

But it was already too late.

And as I walked into my new class and let the heat smack me in the face, I had to wonder if there was anything left to be afraid of.

Mom died when I was four, and I guess I never moved beyond that awful feeling of waking up and the entire world being scary.

I'd had a nighttime routine with Mom. She'd turn on a bedside light that projected stars on my ceiling, and then she'd hold my hand until I fell asleep.

But on the night she died, it was my dad who put me to bed. It was a weird night. She had breast cancer. It moved quickly. The chemo didn't work. And then neither of us knew what to do without her, and I was little and didn't know yet what it meant to be dead and that it was a forever thing. But I knew I was sad that my mom wasn't there, and Dad somehow still managed to turn the stars on for me. Yia Yia was already living with us, so she rocked me until I stopped crying and eventually fell asleep.

Dad slept outside my open bedroom door that night.

He'd dragged a pillow and a blanket into the hallway. Maybe he was lonely. Maybe he wanted to be with us. I don't know. But after that Yia Yia handled bedtime alone. Actually, Yia Yia handled a lot alone. So I don't think it's even possible for me to explain how much it hurt when Yia Yia died last year. It's been quiet.

I like quiet. I really do. But since Yia Yia died it's been unbearably quiet. Not that an old lady made that much more noise, but she took up a lot of space too. She was always running a sewing machine or watching old movies or on the phone or cooking. She wasn't loud per se, but she filled a room. I knew she was there before I heard her, and I guess she filled more than the physical space. She filled my childhood.

Dad didn't know what to do with me. I never wanted to play rough. And I liked being by myself. I cried too much. I was too sensitive. None of that was okay.

Every single thing I did was just a little less than what he wanted, and I knew that without him saying a word. That's how disappointment works. It seeps into you until you know it without hearing the words or seeing the looks. You just feel it in everything the person does, even when someone else watching might not notice. The only thing Dad ever did 100 percent for me was ask Yia Yia to come from Greece and live with us.

He knew I needed her.

After Mom died there was an emptiness. And it's not like Yia Yia's arrival erased the fact that Mom wasn't here anymore, but Yia Yia threw everything she could at the darkness. Until the world didn't seem so dark anymore.

Stories were her weapon of choice.

I think the best thing about Yia Yia was that she told me the things I wasn't exactly supposed to know. And she always told the truth, even if it wasn't what I wanted to hear.

She had other grandkids and family in Greece who wanted her there too, but my dad made a case for her to come here. He said my need was greater, and at the risk of sounding super pathetic, he was right. We agree on this. I needed Yia Yia. I needed someone to listen and love me without question. And Dad knew he couldn't do it, so Yia Yia had to teach me everything.

Yia Yia taught me to swear. She was the one who told me to never, EVER smoke. And she said that with a cigarette in her mouth. She said she'd kill me herself if I ever tried it.

I remember the way her hands felt guiding mine with the yarn.

"Something to keep your hands busy when you get nervous, agapi mou."

And we'd sit there. She'd be in her chair and I'd be on the floor and we'd make stuff together.

Leonidas, let me tell you a story.

Leonidas, let me tell you something.

Leonidas . . .

Even the way she said my name made me feel braver.

She was the one who'd picked it, even though I wished

she hadn't. It's a heavy name to carry. Being named after a warrior who led Spartan men into battle seemed like wishful thinking on her part. Especially since I was not born tough or particularly brave and I mostly just want to knit and take pictures. *Mighty* Leonidas actually has anxiety.

That's why I go to the cemetery to talk to her. I wanted to feel some kind of connection again, something that made me feel braver and stronger—something. The Greek church only recently started allowing cremation, but Yia Yia was old-school. She wanted to be buried in the ground, preferably in Greece, but graveyards in the country are overcrowded, like to the point that a burial is like renting a grave plot for a couple of years. She agreed that was super gross and creepy, so she settled for being buried somewhere close to us.

Mom was cremated, and we scattered her ashes in the ocean. She said she never wanted us visiting a grave site.

So even if family curses are real and bad luck *does* follow lies . . . the worst has already happened, right?

Namaste,
Leo

3

Today's Pose: Downward-Facing Dog

A pose in which I bend over and proudly stick my ass in the air and stare down at my hairy Greek feet and then stare forward at my hairy Greek knuckles.

It is one of the easiest and most-used poses in yoga. Or so I am told. It is how our instructor, Annabelle, tells us we will start our "flow." Which makes me think of peeing.

Everyone in this room has been doing yoga for a while. There's a guy in the corner balancing on his forearms. And another guy in the other corner balancing on his dick.

Okay, no, he's not. But that's the level of the people in this room. They're all good at this. There's an older woman doing some floating Yoda shit and some girls my age standing on their hands like it's no big deal. They like being here, and I very much doubt that any of them started doing yoga as a way of avoiding the manly obligations of their heritage.

But they've accepted me into their group. I almost wish they resented me, because the kindness is overwhelming. If I stumble, someone wants to adjust my pose. If I slow down, someone wants to offer an encouraging nod. I'd feel more comfortable if they just acknowledged the fact that I suck.

Instead, I've become the class pet that everyone is eager to train. Every time I do something remotely correct there's this moment where everyone looks at me like I've fetched the tennis ball for the first time.

Dear Journal,

The journaling part of this really bites. We're supposed to write in the journal before class and after class and every opportunity we get. It's supposed to be a way for us to talk about how we're growing, but I think I'm mostly going to talk about how this shit is weird. Because Annabelle says it's for my eyes only. But she also says we should start each entry writing about new poses first—to chart our "progress." And I guess I can do that.

After yesterday's class, my dad opened the window on our drive home and sat as far away from me as humanly possible in the driver seat, muttering in Greek about the sweat and the smell. But every so often he glanced over at me and nodded. Proudly.

I have no memory of my dad ever looking at me proudly. And it's a little sad that it was in response to my pungent man smell.

But maybe if he knew I was working out on a pink yoga mat in a room mostly full of women or that someone had given me a purple headband because the sweat from my hair was dripping into my eyes . . . Yeah. That would be the end of that special proud moment.

The room looks like it was a dance studio. There's a ballet bar at the front so there's no way it wasn't. Then someone filled it with gongs, rows of LED candles, and Buddha statues chilling in the semidarkness.

It's supposed to be a calming place, and it is, but for some reason that is irritating to me, because I feel like I'm being forced to relax. Then I consider the alternative to being in this room, and I let it go.

Everyone seems to know each other here. They've probably all been doing yoga together for a while, and they have the slightly obnoxious look that healthy people get when they breathe in. Like their air is healthier too.

I take a deep breath in, but all I smell is armpit.

I laid out my mat at the back of the room, as close to the wall as possible.

I would have put it in the far-left corner near the air vent, but we're a small group, and I would have been a really conspicuous outlier all by myself. Also, I tried that already and Annabelle asked me to "join the circle."

She was nice about it, but it still felt like she was

asking me to swear a blood oath and join a cult. A cult of healthy people in yoga pants with fruit floating in their water.

"Welcome and thank you all for being here today to share your glorious energy. Remember that we are doing this at our own pace and that it's important to encourage each other so we can become effective teachers."

Her eyes sort of flicker in my direction, and it's clear by the language Annabelle uses that everyone is meant to ignore the fact that I am terrible and therefore not a great teacher candidate, which is difficult given the amount of falling I do. Even with the easy stuff.

Stand here.

Raise your arms like this.

Lean into the pose.

Deep breaths.

Maybe this is my punishment for lying to Dad.

He dropped me off today, and I know I won't see him until tonight.

It's Wednesday, and I have no idea where he goes. He leaves money on the fridge or takeout on the counter and comes back around nine.

Dad is a translator who works primarily with the Greek consulate in Los Angeles. They refer people to him who need help processing their paperwork. Once in a while he's called in for a court appearance. So maybe Wednesday night is a work thing.

It's probably weird that I don't know where he disappears

to. Or that we never had a conversation about it, but my dad and I don't do talking. We never really had anything to do with each other beyond the occasional checking in about school.

The two-second conversations that give him the information he needs about my life and the ability to exit without getting too involved.

It was something that always bothered Yia Yia. She was the one who organized Christmas gifts, birthday gifts, all our trips to Greece. Without her we would have done even less together, and now that she's gone, we realize how much of our lives existed because of her. The chain-smoking center of our solar system. Fuck cigarettes. Otherwise she'd be here and none of this would be happening.

Also, today was my first meeting with Drake. It should be noted that he looks bigger in small spaces.

And the guidance counselor, Mr. Thomas, told us that we need to work through our issues together as brothers.

Brothers.

He actually said that and I wanted to puke. To be fair, Drake looked like he wanted to puke too. I turned away from him because I don't want to accidentally bond over how stupid we both thought that was.

After twelve minutes of complete silence, Mr. Thomas proclaimed that sometimes you just need to occupy the same space with a person to understand them. Which made me think about the summer I spent with my cousin Demetri, who caught farts in his hands and threw them in my face.

We shared a lot of space that summer, and I am no closer to understanding him.

That's when Mr. Thomas turned on some weird choir music, and Drake and I spent the rest of the time staring at nothing, trying to avoid eye contact completely. Mr. Thomas wears a lot of bright colors, probably because he's the cheer coach and he needs to demonstrate that from space with a neon-yellow polo. He's also one of the younger staff members at school and is a Michael B. Jordan doppelgänger.

This obviously hasn't escaped his notice, because he has an Erik Killmonger bobblehead under his computer monitor.

During the meeting, he would look over at us expectantly, and I would look away, hoping to avoid eye contact with both him AND Drake. Which I did by thinking about Evey.

She probably doesn't remember that time in Greek school when we were the only two students who showed up on a day that class was canceled and had to wait an hour for our parents to drive back and get us. But I do. And as Drake fidgeted in his chair, making annoying squeaking sounds, I thought back to that day to distract myself. I remembered that I'd somehow gotten chocolate from my peanut M&M's on my pants and that I felt the need to cover it up with my backpack when Evey sat down next to me in a white tank top and jean shorts.

My eleven-year-old self had zero chill.

Evey had pulled out one of those paper things that girls fold and you ask it questions. I have no idea what they're called. I don't think anyone knows, but every girl somehow knows how to make them. And we sat there for an hour letting it predict our future.

When our parents finally showed up and I got back in the car, I was about to tell my Yia Yia that according to the fortune-teller paper thing, I was going to get married and have four kids.

That's when Yia Yia shook her head at me gravely and said, "Leave the Paros family alone."

She wouldn't say why, and it seemed like a stupid rule, so I ignored her.

Also, it was hard not to be just a little bit in love with Evey Paros after that day. Which is why I figured out how to fold my own fortune-teller thing and brought it to her at the next class in front of a bunch of the other kids. Not knowing the protocol. Not knowing that I was not cool.

Luckily, she set me straight pretty quick.

She fixed me with a very serious stare, her black eyes locked on mine, and said in a calm, deadly voice, "We are not friends."

So I backed away, and after class I threw my paper fortune-teller away, along with any shred of confidence I'd gained from that afternoon.

It hurt in a strange way. Like I'd spent a lot of time working on a gift that she'd opened and smashed in front of me.

Then I remember thinking later how stupid it had been to walk in front of everyone like that. How innocent. How completely out of character for me. I hadn't realized that Evey was just passing time. That she wasn't being nice to me—she was amusing herself.

The funny thing is, I still have a hard time believing it. We laughed together.

Today, when I checked in for yoga, she acted like she'd never seen me before in her life.

Dark hair, dark eyes, black yoga pants, and a bright blue tank top.

She looked through me as she scanned my card, and there was half a second where I felt like I only really existed because she looked up.

Then I felt pathetic and sidestepped away from the front desk as fast as possible.

Leave the Paros family alone, Yia Yia's voice whispered.

I am trying.

But Evey is Greek. She has two Greek parents. She goes to our Greek Orthodox church every Sunday and has participated in Greek school since she was a kid. So even if I were a hermit who eats bugs alone in the woods (which I mostly am, minus the bug-eating), I still would have known Evey Paros.

Then again, maybe nobody really knows her. Because something happened between summer and Christmas break.

She and Jordan Swansea were a thing at the end of last school year, and even though my general impression of Evey—from a distance, obviously—had been that she was beautiful in a "watch out for the rocks, her song is bewitching you" sort of way, she suddenly became popular as well. She and Jordan were like high school royalty.

Two rich kids who could do no wrong.

Until they broke up.

And I'm sure if I talked to people, I'd know why. I'd probably know a lot more if I talked to people, actually.

I glanced at Drake, now bobbing his head to whatever music was playing from his phone, and considered asking him what had happened between Evey and Jordan. Then, in what I imagined was the middle of some drum solo, he started bobbing his head like he was trying to get water out of his ears. And I changed my mind.

Then the bell rang and I got up to leave Mr. Thomas's office.

"Hey, you dropped this."

It was Drake. He was holding one of my bamboo crochet hooks.

"Thanks," I said, taking out my case and unrolling it to reveal twenty other hooks of various sizes.

Drake watched me with his mouth open, like he couldn't quite explain his level of confusion, before he walked out of the room.

I returned my crochet hooks to my backpack, and my stomach dropped about a foot as my fingers didn't touch the familiar binder that I bring with me everywhere.

It was gone.

My portfolio—all my photos.

GONE.

Namaste,
Leo

4

Dear Journal,

The most honest thing I can write is that my stomach hurts. Always. Without fail. My stomach hurts because I'm nervous. Because I'm hungry. Because I'm talking. Because I'm thinking. It just hurts. That's its response to everything.

My stomach is supposed to, you know, hold food, but instead it has become a warning beacon for the rest of my body, which is absurd because why is my stomach getting this message? Why is my stomach the ambassador of my mental health? But somehow it is, and I need to respect it. And yoga is supposed to help. But I'm not really good at yoga.

Okay, that's a lie. I am a master at child's pose and downward dog. Also corpse pose—I rock that one.

Today Annabelle opened the class by asking us to focus on our strengths. All the things we're good at.

I'm good at appearing to be okay. Projecting normalcy when I don't feel normal.

And this took practice, because every time I feel NOT okay, I hear my dad's voice rise up inside me.

Stop crying, Leo.

Skazmós.

Jesus Christ, every five minutes you're crying about something. Do you see any of the other kids crying? No? Just you.

Yep. Just me.

A guy with anxiety is not part of the phalanx, which is a Greek military formation made up of chiseled naked men holding spears and would not be well served by someone like me, distracted by all the ways I could be killed in battle.

Just you, Leonidas.

It was one of those comments that probably worked for other kids. *Look at them. They're being normal—why aren't you?* And then the kid would stop doing whatever weird thing they were doing and behave.

But it just reminded me that I was incapable of stopping. That I had somehow become the weird thing I was doing.

And that just made me feel worse. The memory of it still stung, even in yoga when I was supposed to be letting my negative energy return to the portals of hell, from whence it came.

Or whatever.

Instead, my mind drifted back to the sparkling conversation in Mr. Thomas's office.

"Dude. Do you have to take a shit?" Drake asked.

Mr. Thomas looked away pointedly, like he wanted to remind Drake not to swear but he also wanted us to keep talking, so he let it go.

"Um, what?"

So maybe I'm not so good at appearing to be normal. Maybe I had been scrunching up my face without realizing it.

Anyway, I should have been used to these kinds of interruptions from Drake, but no one could really prepare for Drake. I took a bite of the prepackaged burrito I'd brought from home and stared at him.

"You look constipated," he said slowly, as if I hadn't heard him.

I was prepared to ignore him again, but he makes it impossible. The room had been dead silent. Mr. Thomas was still pretending not to eavesdrop while he typed something on his computer. And I had been staring at a quote on the wall above his desk, from a poem by Mary Oliver that we'd had to take apart in AP English.

Tell me, what is it you plan to do / With your one wild and precious life?

In the universe of people who like putting quotes on walls, this one is pretty good, but there were other motivational posters around it covered in unicorns and football players and children holding hands that sort of took away from the poem.

Drake was staring at me expectantly like he didn't know

his question was obnoxious. He was leaning back in his chair eating an apple, letting the flecks of juice spray from the fruit as he chomped it like a velociraptor.

Mr. Thomas stopped typing and pretended to be interested in random paperwork on his desk.

"Your face," Drake said. "You look like something hurts or you're trying to take a dump."

"Stomachache," I said.

Drake gave a quick nod as if this answer satisfied his need for information and human contact. Then he eyed my burrito and said, "That burrito is garbage. If you're not constipated now, you will be." Then he tossed me another apple from his bag and leaned back in his chair again with his headphones.

Huge headphones that completely covered his ears, so he couldn't hear me say, "Thank you."

My Yia Yia would have said: *People are not one kind of thing, agapi mou.*

But an apple doesn't mean I want to open up about how my stomach hurts because it's holding every poisonous thought I've ever had.

And despite my dad's stellar supportive attitude, I've learned that worry is okay. There's nothing wrong with worrying about stuff. Everybody does it.

But it isn't just regular worry that takes over my life and beats me over the head with skull-crushing panic.

It's the excessive, persistent worry that takes over. It has power. And it's those repeated episodes of intense fear that really pose a problem. Panic attacks. Anxiety attacks. Those things that immobilize you. You're trapped in a cyclone of worry that you can't reason your way out of and your body, the traitor, responds to it.

Usually with stomachaches. But sometimes, for fun, it's shortness of breath. Sweating. Then it messes with your sleep. Feeling tired is normal too.

Telling someone you're tired is the most boring thing you can say. But for me it's true, because I don't think I ever feel well rested. Even in the morning, when I wake up after eight hours of sleep, I get out of bed and my brain starts running. It's a little bit like being on a treadmill, forever, but you don't want to tell anyone you can't find the switch to turn it off, because you assume everyone is on their own treadmill and they're handling it fine.

Everyone else is always handling it better, I think.

I avoid crowds. Loud noises. Big gatherings. They make me feel like I'm walking through Jell-O and can't run.

There's actually a recurring nightmare I have where everyone starts running. Everyone but me, because I can't. And nobody really knows what they're running from, but they're all able to get away, and I'm trying to lift my feet with my hands because they're stuck. Then I wake up.

In middle school, I tried to figure out what was wrong with me, and I started ruling out all the stuff that I *wasn't* through internet searches.

Even though social situations weren't my favorite, I didn't have a fear of leaving the house or going outside, so agoraphobia was out.

I never found myself unable to speak, so selective mutism was out.

I didn't have specific phobias that I could name, so those were ruled out as well.

Substance-induced anxiety disorder and social anxiety sounded good, but neither of them fit. I wasn't on any substances, and I didn't really engage in enough social activity to deem it a threat to my mental health.

When I started high school, I came across two conditions that made perfect sense. Generalized anxiety disorder and panic disorder.

- **Generalized anxiety disorder** includes persistent and excessive anxiety and worry about activities or events—even ordinary, routine issues. The worry is out of proportion to the actual circumstance, is difficult to control, and affects how you feel physically. It often occurs along with other anxiety disorders or depression.

- **Panic disorder** involves repeated episodes of sudden feelings of intense anxiety and fear or terror that reach a peak within minutes (panic attacks). You may have feelings of impending doom, shortness of breath, chest pain, or a rapid, fluttering, or pounding heart (heart palpitations). These panic attacks may lead to worrying about them happening again or avoiding situations in which they've occurred.

Both could fit, but generalized anxiety fit best. It was like my brain was choosing from a buffet of symptoms and I imagined myself piling it all on a giant platter to carry back to my table.

Feeling nervous, restless, or tense—CHECK.

Having a sense of impending doom—ONLY ALL THE TIME. CHECK!

Having an increased heart rate—CHECK.

Breathing rapidly (hyperventilation)—YUP.

Sweating—YUP.

Trembling—CHECK.

Feeling weak or tired—CHECK.

Having trouble concentrating or thinking about anything other than the present worry—CHECK.

Having trouble sleeping—SOMETIMES YUP.

Experiencing gastrointestinal (GI) problems—ONLY ALWAYS.

Having difficulty controlling worry—DUH.

And I probably could have left it at that with my own self-diagnosis if I hadn't had a minor panic attack during my first (and last) driver's ed class, which ended with me driving into a SLOW CHILDREN AT PLAY sign in the empty parking lot of my old elementary school.

I started sweating and breathing weird, and the instructor called my Yia Yia to come get me.

She made me see a doctor, who confirmed my findings, which I hear is what happens for most people with anxiety.

We already know we're anxious. When we finally go

in to talk to a doctor, it's to determine the degree of our anxiety.

Anyway, that doctor visit was a couple of years ago.

And to be honest, I prefer to have as little to do with doctors as possible. I saw them a lot when Mom was sick. It's their job to deal with sick people, so I get that they can't be super emotionally invested in every patient at every checkup, but the detached look of a doctor doing rounds while your mom is having chemo—that stays with you. And you sort of hope the next doctor might be a little nicer, maybe spend a little more time.

Anyway, Yia Yia wanted me to feel like I had something if I needed it, which is why she talked my dad into letting me try a medication my doctor recommended. I didn't keep taking it, but I have a prescription in case I need it.

The thing is, I don't like drugs. I don't like the light-headed feeling when they don't work right. And I don't like having to rely on something to feel okay. Which is stupid, I guess. But Yia Yia was right: it does make me feel good to have the option when everything gets to be too much.

At the end of that appointment the doctor said I appeared to be handling it well.

Here's the thing, though: it's not really a compliment to tell someone who has anxiety that they don't seem like someone with anxiety. Because it just means we've gotten really good at hiding it. Though, given Drake's reaction earlier today, I think my anxiety is probably a little more obvious than I realized.

And anxiety isn't the kind of thing you can talk to everyone about. The reason I know this is because I remember when my Yia Yia tried to talk to my dad about it.

He told her I needed to just stop it. That I was whining and just trying to keep her attention.

Attention-seeking.

Because it's so glamorous, right? It's probably the reason most people don't want to admit they're dealing with it. Like I feel better about myself because I have anxiety and I need to tell someone else so they can feel sorry for me? No, actually, that's not it. I wouldn't tell anyone if I could help it. In fact, I don't tell anyone. When I start feeling overwhelmed, I just sort of shrink into myself and stop talking for a while. I don't make a production of it, and I don't try to include anyone on this very special tour of my nerves.

But my Yia Yia noticed everything. And she didn't exactly come from a background that prescribed drugs and therapy. But she loved me, so she found other ways to help. Hence the yarn and the matis. Because she thought the evil eye could definitely help keep the bad stuff away.

But it's personal too. My anxiety is not the same as someone else's anxiety. And I don't want to be told what I need to do to handle it.

I guess Dad just didn't know what to do either. He still doesn't. We sit next to each other in church once a week because that's the one thing we still do even though Yia Yia isn't around to make us do it. The Sunday after she died we both got dressed without her, and for a second we both forgot that she was gone, and neither of us wanted to admit that. So we just went to church. Sat next to each other for an hour. And left.

Which is nice. It's something we both do at the same time. But I wouldn't exactly call it something we do together. It's just sharing space.

Namaste,
Leo

5

Today's Pose: Crow

This is another inversion, which means you go upside down. Or you have the potential to, at least. The goal of the pose is to have your knees rest delicately on your upper arms.

You start in downward dog and walk your feet forward until your knees touch your arms.

Bend your elbows.

Lift heels off floor.

Rest knees against the outside of your upper arms.

It's not as impossible as it sounds, because I've actually seen other students do it, but there's also the somewhat distracting moment when someone loses their balance and face-plants into a puddle of their own sweat and the rest of the class has to keep their positions while someone—me—struggles to untangle their legs and try again.

And I've mentioned the sweat, but I haven't really mentioned the sweat. Not to the point that anyone who hasn't taken a hot yoga class can fully understand.

At the start of class, someone takes a giant mop and soaks up all the sweat from the previous class and then jumps on a towel to dry the rest of the residual wetness on the floor. Once you're finished throwing up thinking about that, you start your class.

About half an hour into the class, our mats look like tiny islands floating in sweat again.

Other people's sweat touches you. You step in it on the way out the door.

It is everywhere, but no one says anything about it because they're over it.

Everyone except for me.

Dear Journal,

My mind is still thrumming in a steady wave of panic as I mentally retrace my steps and try to think of every possible location where my portfolio might be.

I tore my room apart at home, retraced my steps through all my classes, and even walked through the quad area at lunch, thinking I might have dropped it on my way to the parking lot.

Then I stopped dead when I saw Evey standing there by the lunch tables surrounded by people.

I rarely see her at school. We exist in the same ecosystem of people, but I'm more like algae in her world, if that makes any sense—gross, smelly algae just kind of existing.

Then, to up the weirdness factor, she was talking to Drake. It was like some strange crossover episode of my life as they both turned to look at me at the same time, and instead of walking away casually, I did a double take and walked into a trash can.

It's one of those embarrassing moments that I'll revisit ten years from now, but for today it'll just be the thing distracting me in yoga as I go through the motions as if I have completely forgotten how to walk, stand, sit, and appear human.

Annabelle asks us to think about what brings us to our mats today, and I'm pretty sure I'm supposed to say my mental well-being or a desire to bond with the universe, but the truth is: avoidance.

Avoidance brings me to my mat today.

I am actively avoiding the class down the hall and also my dad, the big Greek guy in the Toyota Corolla out front, probably cleaning his ears with his car keys.

Annabelle asks us to listen to our bodies and to take a moment to appreciate our physical forms and our tremendous strength, and all I can think about is how I walk with my stomach muscles clenched and about how it has nothing to do with my physical strength. I don't remember when I started doing it, bracing myself for a punch, but now that's just how my stomach is. And it isn't just when I'm around other people or doing something new. It is all the time. Everything feels tight and constricted, like I have to hold on to my organs or they'll come spilling out of me in a disgusting, bloody mess on the floor.

Annabelle stands about two feet from me at all times because I need so much attention, and not one person seems irritated by this. It's as if helping me NOT suck is part of the karmic energy of yoga.

She asked me if it was okay to reach out and reposition me, and I said yes, so now she moves my arms like I'm some weird marionette and puts her hands on my legs and back and calves and neck to show me how I'm supposed to move.

The touch doesn't bother me. The fact that I need so much guidance and that my body is, like, completely unresponsive to everything I ask it to do—that part is annoying. I can't even bend over all the way and touch my toes.

That was surprising. But I guess if you have no need to bend over and touch your toes all the time, you don't check it out to make sure you still can.

For half a second it takes my mind off my current mental meltdown.

There are moments when my anxiety takes center stage in my life. There are moments when it completely consumes me. To an extent I actually agree with my dad, because why can't I control my own head and why are my thoughts capable of destroying me?

All the worst-case scenarios for my missing portfolio are savagely attacking my brain with tiny pinpricks of panic.

For other people this might be a classic *C'mon, guys, let's retrace your steps* moment, but for me it is a gigantic schism in my brain. Half of me knows that this can't possibly be the worst thing to ever happen, and the other half is a rat fighting with a squirrel for a piece of cardboard covered in melted cheese.

Which is why I mostly attribute this and everything else that sucks in my life to bad luck.

And a curse that has plagued our family for years and was, until recently, the only distant connection I've had to Evey Paros.

Here's the short version of the story:

My great-great-grandfather Stavros was a thief who made off with a lot of priceless heirlooms from the village we're from. And he mostly got away with it.

Until he got caught. By Evey's great-great-grandmother Evriklia, who noticed him stealing a small religious icon from their home. A tiny hand-painted portrait of Mary and Jesus in a gold frame.

Evriklia told everyone that he was a thief, but Stavros actually got the village to believe she was crazy—an old woman making things up.

So, naturally, she cursed him.

Looked him straight in the eye and said, "I hope you burn in hell. The devil can have you for the lies you've told."

Then she spit on the ground at his feet. And he laughed. Laughed like a big stupid fucking idiot because he knew

44

he'd gotten away with it, which seems insane because living with Yia Yia has made me kind of an expert on old Greek women—and when they say something, I believe them.

Anyway, the bastard died two weeks later in a fiery car crash. Not exactly hell, but there was definitely burning involved, and our family has never been the same since.

Thus, the beginning of the curse.

And it may have been more likely that Stavros died because he was not a great driver and the white mule he swerved to avoid had appeared quickly around a sharp corner, or so the story goes . . . but either way, our family has made a concerted effort to avoid lies and the Paros family ever since.

Unfortunately, bad luck has always found a way in, and anytime something went wrong in our house, Yia Yia would shake her fist to the ground and yell, "Ai gamisou re Stavro."

Translation: Fuck Stavros.

If she was feeling particularly angry she'd call him "Koproskyla tou kerata."

Shithound of the devil.

Which seems appropriate.

So, yes. Fuck Stavros. It has to be his fault that my portfolio is gone.

I continue to dwell on all the ways the missing portfolio could destroy my life, how all the photographs are out in the open for other people to see and judge and how I am nothing without them because, contrary to what my dad thinks, they are important.

Mom would have understood.

Having them out in the world without context is really terrifying.

Then yoga class ended and my exhausted body accepted fatigue.

Until Evey Paros came over to me and handed me a note that read:

> I think I found something that belongs to you.
> Let's talk about these photos. Grindz after
> class. But shower first.
>   Evey

So I could breathe again. Almost.

But the fear of losing my portfolio morphed into the fear that Evey had seen all my photos.

And also, what could she possibly want to talk about?

I know I have to keep writing in this thing because that's what everyone else is doing on their mats, but I'm not sure how much of this is going to be about yoga, so I feel the need to apologize about that in advance.

> Namaste,
> Leo

Today's Pose: ????

Some animal pose that looks like a squatting toad. I'm not paying attention, so naturally I fall a lot. But no worse than usual.

Dear Journal,

Today I am ignoring yoga. I am sorry.

It's just that my mind is elsewhere. My focus is no longer in tune with my developing yogi spirit (okay, it was really never with my developing yogi spirit) because I'm still thinking about what it was like to have coffee with Evey Paros.

I told Dad I was going to meet up with some friends, and

he didn't question it, even though a huge bushy eyebrow was raised in my direction.

I'd never been to Grindz before, but I knew where it was. Everyone from school went there. Plus, it was two streets over from the gym.

When I got there, I realized I didn't know what to order. I don't drink coffee, so I opted for a juice and a cookie.

Evey came in about five minutes later, ordered a latte, and then walked over to my table as if she'd already noticed I was there. Even though I hadn't seen her eyes flick toward me.

She held her coffee in her hand, and I set my cookie on the table with my glass of juice (some weird pear flavor) and then realized how stupid I looked by comparison.

She pulled out my portfolio, and I sighed with such deep relief that my whole body unclenched for a second.

But then she put her hand on top of it and pulled it back toward her.

I wasn't exactly making it difficult for her to read my body language when I practically leaned forward to follow my portfolio across the table. She smirked a little as she opened it to start turning pages to the spots she'd marked with Post-it notes.

"These are good," she said. "I could use something like this." My chest lifted at her words. I started to form a question, but I didn't even get the words out of my mouth before she spoke again. "I think your photography might be the perfect way to get back at my ex-boyfriend."

I told her I didn't understand, and it seemed to take a

great deal of restraint on her part to keep from telling me exactly how stupid I was.

She handed me the flyer for the photo contest I'd folded into my portfolio.

"This doesn't have to be unpleasant. We can help each other. I'm trying to create some imagery for someone who deserves to be punished," she said. "I want to work with you to stage some photographs that we can use to teach him a lesson."

"What kind of less—?"

Her eyes darkened and I stopped talking. There was something oddly powerful about the way she commanded silence. The confidence that surrounded every movement. It was awe-inspiring. Like she saw everything I was trying to hide and was embarrassed for me.

Evey flipped through some of the pages a little more aggressively than I would have liked and landed on a familiar brightly colored page in a sea of black-and-white. She pointed to a set of photos where there was yarn draped over two trees and wrapped around a bench. In my head, I'd always called them my Colorful Death collection because it was the first time I'd taken pictures at the cemetery. And the first time I'd yarn-bombed.

I wanted to reach out and grab the portfolio back, not necessarily because that photo was so personal but because I'd taken it at the cemetery near my house, where Yia Yia is buried.

I actually took a bunch of them there, and I wasn't really

in the mood to be told how morbid it was to take artsy yarn pictures next to tombstones and mausoleums.

I also wasn't prepared to hint at how much time I spend there just knitting and taking pictures. Knitting with dead people is weird. I get it.

"What is this?" she asked, pointing. "You knit?"

Maybe she hadn't noticed the tombstones in the back of the black-and-white shots.

"And crochet," I told her.

"Interesting. That works nicely," she said.

She continued to flip through my portfolio, and I hated how quickly she moved her fingers over every picture, but more than that, I hated how much I held my breath while she did it. No one had ever seen my work before. Not my dad. Not my Yia Yia. No one.

Showing my dad would have been a little bit like offering him a macaroni necklace.

"There's a lot in here that doesn't interest me," she said. She wasn't even trying to be mean; she was just stating a fact. Like she was conducting business.

I tried to think up some response to that. Something clever and direct that I wouldn't stay up all night regretting later, but then she interrupted my thoughts.

"These are exceptional."

I didn't expect that response and was annoyed by how much I perked up at her approval. My eyes traveled down to where her index finger tapped the page. It was one I'd done right after Yia Yia died. Yarn everywhere. Brilliant colors cascading down her tombstone and over the park bench facing her grave. I frowned.

"It's yarn-bombing," I told Evey, reaching out for the portfolio. It was something I'd discovered by accident after Yia Yia died. I'd been knitting at the cemetery, working on a yellow beanie, and it wasn't until I'd made it halfway home that I realized I'd left it behind.

What was even more annoying was that it wasn't on the bench where I'd been sitting, or on the ground either. I wandered the cemetery for over an hour looking for it because I was pissed that I'd somehow managed to lose it. Also, I didn't want to go home to a fridge full of food from church people. Eventually I found it on the head of a statue near the entrance. Before I yanked it off, some guy with flowers who must have been visiting a grave walked by and shook his head, saying, "Who yarn-bombs a cemetery?"

That's when I Googled it and found all the pictures of yarn covering random crap. Benches. Lampposts. A tank. People did other amazing things with it too. I'd seen photos online of giant yarn spiderwebs hanging across public buildings.

I reached out again for the portfolio.

"And that photo is private. It's—"

"Your grandmother. I know," she said softly, tugging it back. "So are you in or not?"

"What if I don't want to?" I asked, and before the words even left my mouth, I knew I was stuck.

She smiled, and even though she didn't say it out loud,

her narrowed eyes said very clearly: *I'll make sure your dad finds out about yoga.*

Whatever tiny bubble of happiness had formed in my stomach popped. I wasn't sure exactly how she knew that would be devastating for me. Probably my expression when I asked her to move me on the first day. Maybe it was the way my voice cracked. That was probably really obvious to someone who looks for other people's weaknesses.

The awful thing is, she was right. She saw my weakness immediately and exploited it.

The thought of being sent to Greece to live with my fart-throwing cousin who likes to tangle all my yarn and "pretend" to drop my camera equipment filled me with a hot, sticky feeling of dread. The kind that forces my stomach to clench over and over again.

When I said nothing, her smile was cold.

"Like I said, this doesn't need to be unpleasant. We can help each other. And there are a few things I'll need from you. . . ."

She pulled out the photo contest flyer and highlighted the portion I hadn't completed yet, the part that asked for a theme for the portfolio submission.

Before I could open my mouth or tell her I was out or do anything other than stare at her, she said, "Your theme can be revenge." She leaned back in her chair, waving her hands enthusiastically as she spoke. "And the photos are going to be creative and devastating, with hidden messages.

But visually stunning, of course. And when we're done we'll post them all at the same time."

She smiled at me again as if she'd just handed me some dream assignment, but I couldn't wrap my head around being an accomplice to this. Jordan Swansea was probably an asshole, but he'd never done anything to me. Weren't people usually pissed after a breakup, and how could I possibly get in the middle of this epic shitstorm?

I stared at my portfolio and the flyer that had been hanging out of it, trying to reason my way out of this. Then Evey leaned in and whispered, "E tan e epi tas."

Even non-Greeks know that means "Return with your shield or on it."

Again I was annoyed at how that lifted me ever so slightly. It was the only time she'd mentioned some kind of connection between us. We're both Greek. We both speak the language. Technically. Even though there's no doubt that Evey is way better at speaking it than I am.

I always think in English first because that golden language window was sort of wasted when my mom got sick.

Yia Yia made sure I was conversant in Greek, but I really should have started in Greek school when I was a toddler, like everyone else. Dad's priorities were, you know, elsewhere. You might even say he was a born-again Greek after Mom died because he was trying to bring us back to some kind of normal. Like normal was even a possibility.

But Yia Yia helped. She was the one who made sure I could speak Greek and read it. She never said it had to be perfect, but there was no way I was going to make excuses about not being able to speak it.

"Leonidas, you were named for a Greek warrior. You will speak your native language."

And I didn't argue with Yia Yia.

But Evey has two parents who speak it at home. And even though it was spoken a lot in my house, there was some kind of disconnect in my brain that made my speech sound a little bit like a four-year-old's.

I will never forget the time I asked to go to the bathroom at Greek school and everyone laughed because I'd said, "If I may please the toilet."

Hilarious.

It would have been poetic. Our two families working together to accomplish something.

Absolutely poetic. If one of us weren't being blackmailed to do it.

She handed me my portfolio, and my hand grazed hers when I reached out to take it. There was a moment when her eyes darted to the spot where our hands had touched and then she decided to pretend nothing had happened.

Her hands were cold, and I was not surprised.

"So you really hate this guy," I said. I thought I was saying something obvious, but instead of agreeing with me, Evey looked at me like I'd just said something painfully stupid.

"I don't hate anyone," she said coldly. "Hate is passion. And Jordan Swansea doesn't deserve that." Then she grabbed her phone off the table and said, "We'll talk soon."

I didn't even get the chance to ask, "Hey, if he was such a bad guy, why'd you date him for so long? Didn't you figure out pretty early that he was trash?"

What I did manage to squeak out before she left was "Is this because of the curse?"

She flicked her hair over her shoulder as her Greekness blasted me in the face because it was the exact same expression my grandmother would have worn if she'd been calling me an idiot.

It was a look that conveyed anger, but in a way that celebrated the anger. Like it was a powerful weapon.

And for a second I thought she was going to tell me I was delusional, but her mouth twisted into a smile and she said, "Oxi."

Which means "no" in Greek. Which told me she absolutely was invoking the mysterious power of the curse here.

"Are you in?" she asked.

I knew I didn't have a choice. Not really, anyway.

"Yeah, I'm in," I said.

"Good. Tell no one. What's your number?" she asked, opening her contacts list. I told her and she entered it and sent me a text: *Hi.*

"Perfect. See you at rehearsal," she said.

"Oh, right."

I had completely blocked the March 25 Greek Independence Day pageant rehearsal from memory. It commemorates the Greek freedom from the Turks. In Greece it's huge, and it's a pretty big deal in the Unites States too.

It's an opportunity for all Greeks to come together to celebrate their Greekness.

Small children practice the language by memorizing poems. Everyone eats. And everyone sings the national anthem. And of course there's the dancing.

But in addition to being painfully boring, it's also, now, a little bit depressing.

The March 25 pageant at our church reminds me, a young Greek man, that as a descendant of warriors, I can only assume that I would have been left on a mountaintop somewhere as an offering to whatever god collects the babies who cannot defend Sparta.

Hephaestus maybe? I don't imagine it's a super-desirable god job.

When I left Grindz, Dad had sent me a text message: *There are vegetables in the fridge.*

I'm not sure what he expected me to do with said vegetables, but I suppose the intent there was for me to eat something that was not prepackaged or covered in cheese.

There was definitely an effort being made, so I did feel a little guilty ignoring the vegetables completely and heating up a frozen pizza instead.

Namaste,
Leo

7

Today's Pose: Cat and Cow

In this case, cat pose means you arch your back like a cat hissing. Cow pose means you drop your stomach and raise your ass high into the air again.

Most yoga poses seem to be about raising your ass to the heavens, then dropping it back to earth delicately in the name of exercise.

Dear Journal,

It was about an hour after we had coffee together that Evey started sending me text messages. This was strange because usually I only get texts from Dad and Tangled Yarn Barn because Dad feels obligated to inform me of his where-abouts and Tangled Yarn Barn has me by the balls with their 50-percent-off-all-merchandise sale that includes their pricier yarns.

Screw your judgment, Journal. Cashmere is expensive.

Anyway, Evey's first few texts were the following:

> Can you tell me what
> other stuff you can knit?

> Do you have stuff already
> made that you could
> use if you needed to?

> Are you afraid of dogs?

I sent a few pictures of some yarn projects to answer her first question and responded *Yes* to the second. Then I wanted to respond to the third random question with *Yes, if they're trying to bite my face off, I will most definitely crap myself,* but instead I replied, *Nope. Not afraid of dogs.*

She responded with:

> Great. Get it all ready. I'll
> let you know when we're
> doing the first photo.

My stomach clenched and I had a bad feeling about this, even as I walked into yoga and handed the gym attendant—not Evey today—my card.

As I walk into class, it occurs to me how yoga studios are *everywhere* in California. You can't walk into a Target without seeing a literal shrine to stretchy pants. That's just the culture.

I'm back middle, and I put my water bottle at least a foot away from my mat on one side and my folded extra towel at least a foot away on my other side.

If I don't do this, people encroach on my space and I can smell them the minute the room starts to heat up.

Class starts, and after a few minutes that involve some breathing exercises and a few almost-face-plants, I glance up into the mirror to see that, thanks to Annabelle's patient guidance, I am standing like everyone else. Then I notice the sweat that has pooled across the front of my sweatpants and down my legs and realize that I look like I've pissed myself.

Awesome.

Guess that's why everyone is wearing tight black pants.

I close my eyes and then squint through them to look around.

I am now the only guy in this class. Apparently, the others were visiting yogis looking for a place to practice (as you do). Hence the presence of the guy balancing on his dick (not really) and the other equally impressive tall guy with muscles as big as my face.

After a while, we're invited to practice our favorite poses or work on something we're trying to master.

I don't have a favorite pose, and I'm trying to master everything. Actually, anything.

So I end up choosing child's pose but lay my cheek on my towel and turn my head to watch everyone else.

There's a blond white girl to my right named Stephanie doing a perfect handstand, and two black girls, twins a little older than me, directly in front of me taking turns spotting each other as they complete some complicated pose that I will never be able to do. From eavesdropping on their conversation, I know that the one with the braids is Nicole and the one wearing the army-green tank top is Tara. They said on the first day of class that they wanted to open a yoga studio together. A Latina girl named Damaris usually sits in the center of her mat with earbuds in before every class. Iris lies on her back, staring up at the ceiling, taking deep breaths, and three girls—Tiffany, Bri, and Catherine—are the only people in the room interrupting the silence. Then there's an old white lady named Carol, who looks like her body might float off the ground at any moment. Like Yoda. She just has that look of someone who knows what they're doing. So maybe this teacher training is something she's doing for fun. Then Annabelle. Then me. And that's it.

Even with my one-foot buffer on each side, the flying sweat is incredible. And I never expected that to be a thing. I never expected to want space because I was afraid of other people's sweat landing on my face. Because if anyone moves too exuberantly, it happens, and you get used to it, but it's not any less gross.

The room is an actual swamp, and 100 degrees is probably exactly what hell is like. But every so often I hear the door open down the hall and a crowd of guys running to the drinking fountains like a heard of wildebeests, and I know I made the right choice, even though my current situation is definitely an example of my bad luck.

Yia Yia was always worried about bad luck. More specifically, *my* bad luck.

She read my cards a lot, which for some reason really irritated my dad, so she did it when he was out of the house.

And it wasn't like Harry Potter, where she saw the Grim and predicted my death or anything. But whatever the cards turned up didn't please her. She'd look at them, then look at me like I wasn't even trying to attract good luck. I never got the specifics of her findings, but I could tell that whatever she'd discovered was not ideal. She always wanted to read my cards and get glimpses into my future, but I think she also had this weird belief that no one should know too much about their own future.

The vague predictions she did give were always the same.

She saw something in front of me. Some vague, gigantic, unrecognizable shape, and the cards always pointed to change. Something she thought would alter the course of my life.

So it became an obsession with her. Trying to see what was ahead so she could protect me from it.

She was trying to spare me from any more pain. But now I've lost her too.

And I wondered what she'd say to me right now if I told her what was going on with Evey.

Probably that I should have listened to her and stayed away from the Paros family.

But even with Yia Yia's dire warning hanging over my head, there would have been no way for me to avoid the Paros family completely. Evey goes to my school. Her parents are the biggest contributors to the church. Maria Paros, Evey's mom, is on every Greek scholarship committee the Hellenic Association has. Therefore, when Yia Yia said avoid them, what she meant was avoid them as much as possible.

Because Stavros screwed us all.

So there's that.

And I'm not sure how much of this I believe. Curses are literally words that a person says to another person. If we were so concerned about that, we might swear less in traffic. If words in general held any power at all, then my mom would still be alive. And my Yia Yia would still be alive because she would have stopped smoking when I asked her to.

But you need more than words to protect people. At least, Yia Yia thought so.

She used to tuck matis into my clothes when I was little. My first worry beads were a chain of tiny Greek eyeballs. Which sounds totally grotesque here but is totally normal in Greece. And even though my Yia Yia was very much a churchgoing woman, she still believed in curses and luck and the unbelievable power of old Greek women.

Strictly speaking, matis weren't a Greek Orthodox thing

originally. They're all over, actually, and really popular in the Mediterranean and West Asia. And like I said, they've been co-opted, and there's no denying that they have a distinct pagan feel. Still, I've never actually been into a Greek house that didn't have a big blue eye hanging somewhere.

We should just be praying for protection, right? Not hanging up an eyeball to ward off bad luck. There's a prayer called the xematiasma that Yia Yia used to do, but it's really long, so first she'd have to check and see if it was necessary.

She'd fill a cup with a little bit of water and another bowl with a little bit of oil and she'd say, "In the name of the Father, the Son, and the Holy Spirit—for Leonidas." And then she'd make the sign of the cross over the water three times. Then she'd say, "Jesus Christ arise and scatter all evil work," and she'd pour one drop of the olive oil into the water. She'd repeat this two more times. The way it's supposed to work is that if the drops of oil stick together into one big blob, it means the person you're trying to pray for has the evil eye. If the oil remains in the water as three separate drops, then they're okay.

But to be honest, I don't think there was ever a time when she didn't just have a giant blob floating in water, which is how she became convinced that I always had the eye on me. For her, this just meant she had to be extra vigilant with prayers.

She had all the Saint Days memorized and we still followed all the regular Anglo superstitions about broken mirrors and open umbrellas, but she was very careful about weird Greek superstitions too. No cutting your fingernails at night or on Fridays because that's bad luck. And no handing someone a pair of scissors or a bar of soap because it means you'll have a fight with them.

Then she'd tell me and my dad that when our hands itched we'd be getting money or that when we spilled salt we needed to throw it over our shoulder to keep the devil away.

But Death came twice to our family already. Maybe he's done with us for a while. Maybe our luck is due for a change.

Yia Yia would have said that unexpected kindness was the only way to strike back against bad luck. She used to say it confused the devil, who assumed people would just crumble when their lives went down the toilet.

Unexpected kindness, I thought.

I was walking out of yoga when I noticed that Evey had arrived and was sitting at the front desk alone. She had her legs crossed in her office chair and she was looking at her phone with a serious expression on her face. No doubt plotting whatever horrible thing she was going to ask me to help her with.

It was a little bit like approaching something potentially dangerous. Not a venomous snake or a bear or anything that's just scary by nature. But like, maybe something that has the potential to be dangerous, so you keep your distance. Like a peacock maybe. Beautiful, obviously, but they can be pretty vicious and territorial.

I decided that I wasn't going to be any weirder than

usual, but I also wasn't going to pretend to be invisible. I was going to be me. And if my luck was bad, then I was going to change it myself.

That's when I remembered that I had tucked something into my bag a while back for a yarn project I hadn't finished.

When I passed her desk, I set it on the AP English binder she'd left open, and walked away.

She held up the crocheted rose and called out, "What is this for?"

"For luck," I said, shrugging.

And in reality, it probably won't change anything. But a smile is generally a good sign, right?

Namaste,
Leo

Today's Pose: Shavasana, or Corpse Pose

Do nothing.

Think of nothing.

Play dead.

This is the pose we end every class with, and it makes sense because death seems like a natural end to a class where you're forced to sweat in an inferno with a bunch of strangers.

But I have to admit there's actually something nice about it too.

It's quiet. Your heart rate starts to shift back to normal, and you listen to all the gross squishy things in your body take a break from whatever they were just doing to keep you alive. Everything pauses and everyone is still. For a few

minutes, you don't feel like you're sucking someone else's
sweat through your nose.

And then somewhere in the quiet Annabelle rings a tiny
little gong and whispers:

"Death is just a pause."

Which is some really deep shit.

Then everyone slowly peels themselves off their mats, and
we stumble out of the room like zombies into the temperature-
regulated gym. Trying to adjust to the light after our recent
journey into death.

Dear Journal,

I am never late for anything. It's one of those anxiety things
that makes me feel like I have some degree of control. If I
can get to a place when I say I'm going to be there, then I
can check off that box. But if there's a chance I will be late,
I get anxious and I can feel my body counting down until
I get to where I'm supposed to be.

My brain will say something like: *I have seven minutes to*
leave and still get there in plenty of time. I have three minutes
to leave and still get there in plenty of time. I have thirty seconds to
leave and still get there in plenty of time.

Luckily, my dad and I have this in common. He's never
late for anything either. And since he is still driving me to
what he believes is a class that is going to teach me some
superhero-level fighting shit, at least I don't have to worry
about being late.

He doesn't wait in the car anymore, though. He drops me off and comes back to get me. And on Wednesdays I still have no idea where he goes.

I just get text messages like this from him instead: *Soup from Anna Papadalos in the fridge.*

Mrs. Papadalos is one of the last holdouts of the church people who brought homemade stuff over after Yia Yia died. But she also has cats. And there is a high chance that the soup is half fur. So I sent him a thumbs-up and made a mental note to grab a sandwich from next door after class before heading to the front desk.

Today, Evey did that thing where she pretended she'd never seen me before when she scanned my card. I was like a ghost who'd slipped into the gym.

Not weird at all. Especially since we'd just had a full conversation via text the day before.

So I left a crocheted daisy on her keyboard and walked to yoga without looking back.

Okay, *conversation* might be a bit strong. She'd sent me a bunch of photos of yarn projects and asked if I could make them, and I'd told her yes.

They were small projects and fairly quick to finish, so it hadn't seemed like a problem.

She'd responded with *He won't know what hit him.*

And guilt pooled in the pit of my stomach like acid as I tugged at my new clothes.

I'd had to buy two pairs of men's yoga pants. There were a few color options and some that clung a little bit more than the pants I was used to wearing, but I didn't really want my balls on display. So I just opted for something I knew I could sweat in.

Ironically not sweatpants, as I'd discovered. Those aren't for actual sweat. Those are for dads to do grocery shopping.

I also walked past Drake on my way into hot yoga, and he saw without saying a word, which was not like him at all. Especially since we'd had one of our meetings this afternoon and it was a sparkling success that went something like this:

Drake: So do you want to talk?

Me: No.

Drake: Dude, we're supposed to talk.

Me: So talk to yourself.

AND HE FUCKING DOES.

He starts talking to himself in the most obnoxious way possible because he is the most obnoxious human being on the planet.

"Well, since you won't talk to me," he says to the wall, "guess we're stuck here. And it's not like I actually wanted to hit you. It was a mistake. I just reacted. Badly. And now we're here. Together. Not talking about brotherhood and shit."

I want to tell him that when I was knitting and not bothering anyone, it wasn't on the same level as smacking someone in the face, but I was happier not speaking.

But Drake was not. He cleared his throat and unleashed a flood of information.

"I could be eating carne asada tacos with Jen or studying

for my algebra test, which I really should be doing, or shooting hoops or doing pretty much anything else, but here I am. In this room with you. Sitting still."

It seemed like it was causing him physical pain to stay in one place. His foot bounced up and down against the desk in front of him and made a sound like cymbals that even seemed to bug Mr. Thomas. I'm not sure Drake realizes how loud he is.

Like when he settles himself into a chair, I can hear every single creak of the metal, and every sound he makes when his body comes into contact with furniture. He taps his pen on the desk and then smiles at me because he knows it's annoying, but luckily Mr. Thomas finally steps in and stops him.

He tells Drake he can listen to music and says for the second time, "Sometimes it's just important to share the same space, and we don't always need to speak for progress to happen."

Sure, dude. I wonder if that's how he handles cheer practice.

Drake might be the kind of guy who just needs to annoy somebody. He likes to push other people's buttons, and even if the response is negative, he enjoys it.

Mr. Thomas gets this. He knows exactly what kind of person Drake is. There's no way you could sit in the same room and not understand this about him within five minutes, but the difference is that Mr. Thomas seems to genuinely enjoy our meetings. He wants everybody to love everybody, so anytime he has the opportunity to put two people in a room, it becomes his life mission to create a bond.

After five minutes, I pulled my knitting needles out of my backpack because screw that guy, and this is how it went.

Me: *Pulls out yarn and knitting needles*

Drake: You're going to do that shit again?

Me: Yep.

Drake: Aren't you embarrassed?

Me: No.

Drake: Well, I'm embarrassed for you.

Me: Good use of your time.

I turned back to the scarf I was working on and tuned him out. We spent the rest of the time avoiding each other, and Mr. Thomas seemed mildly disappointed that Drake hadn't yet annoyed me enough to start up a conversation. Even an angry one. Because then at least that would have been something to work with. Something that would create a starting point for our "journey to brotherhood."

And that's when I started to think about how I'm going on a lot of journeys these days.

Surprisingly, my yoga journey is the only one going well.

I thought the heat would kill me and it would be better to just admit that I lied to my dad and accept my fate, but I actually . . . feel good doing it?

But it is still two hours of hot yoga. It's one of the few moments when you realize that your eyebrows actually serve the biological purpose of keeping sweat and other crap out of your eyeballs.

And my skin, which I think was dry about 85 percent of the time, has taken on this permanent dewy state. I'm told by the other yogis in my class (shut up, that's what we call each other) that I have removed a shit ton of toxins from my body.

It also makes you hyperaware of all the stuff your body is doing. Like I never thought about the back of my knee before, but when you have to do gorilla pose and you hang your head as low as you can and it bumps your knee, sometimes you hold the back of your leg and you find a weird scar you forgot you had. And it reminds you that your body is basically a map of all your physical experiences.

Then, while I was knitting and Mr. Thomas was working at his desk, my phone buzzed with a series of texts from Evey. And even though phones aren't allowed in class, I took a risk and texted back, assuming Mr. Thomas wouldn't mind, since this technically isn't a class. Drake sat up with interest, which I can only assume is because he thinks I'm a cave dweller with limited connection to the outside world.

Do you have bright red yarn?

Yep.

What other colors do you have?

All of them.

Would it be hard to knit a bra?

I thought about this for a second and imagined my dad walking in on me knitting a bra.

> Not really. When do you need it?

> As soon as possible. Can it be huge and embarrassing?

But then something tugged uncomfortably at me.

> Look. I'm still in, but I need a reason this guy deserves this. Something specific.

I expected her to text back immediately, but she didn't respond.

So my world went quiet again. Which was a relief, since going to yoga and having meetings with Drake were the most social interactions I'd had in a long time. And it was exhausting. PEOPLE are exhausting. Keeping up with their conversations and lives. Their likes and dislikes. It's like an endless spiral of things that don't interest me.

Sometimes it just makes me realize how much I don't mind being alone. I swear.

It's something that everyone is constantly trying to fix in me. My Yia Yia was desperate for me to do something, ANYTHING, with other children, and I never wanted to. It was always a battle. She tried a bunch of different things.

Like signing me up for gymnastics, which ended in disaster when I sprained my ankle flying off a tiny trampoline.

Or soccer, which was okay because when you're little you can just sit down in the middle of the field and eat an orange at the end and no one cares, except your dad, who covers his face in shame.

Then I think Yia Yia had a moment where she just decided to let me be weird and worried and anxious. And that's when she taught me to knit.

But I get that it would be better for me as a human if I learned to make friends properly. It's a biological need to be around other people, I guess. A reminder that we were once cavepeople who relied on each other for survival.

But since we don't anymore, I don't see what the big deal is if I want to be left alone.

It is a big deal, Yia Yia would say. *Because love matters. No one can love you if you hide all the time.*

And then I'd tell her I'm not really hiding—I'm just waiting for the right person to find me.

Then she'd stare at me and go back to her room to pray some more, and I'd find a few extra matis stuffed in my backpack.

Evey still hadn't texted back, so I figured she was just irritated by the question. But then when I got out of the shower there were two texts on my phone. One was a photo of a skinny white kid with brown hair and acne. His shiny braces were fully exposed over a wide, toothy smile.

This is Milo Harris.

Jordan got the water polo team to lock him in a porta-potty and tip it over. After that Jordan and the rest of the team took every opportunity to mess with Milo. He had to switch schools. This is just one of the things I've found out so far. Believe me there's more.

OK . . . that's specific.

I'd known Milo Harris. He was supposed to be my lab partner freshman year, then disappeared after two months of school. Now I knew why.

Bad people do not just show up one day as bad people. They have been bad people their whole lives and either they are really good at hiding it or other people have been making excuses for them. Or both.

And you didn't know this while you were dating him?

I sent it before I thought about the full meaning of my words. That she had knowingly ignored awful things about someone she was in a relationship with. But then I saw that she was starting to type.

> I didn't want to know then. And I was one of the people making excuses for him.

> Are you still in?

How big do you want the bra?

> ENORMOUS.

> Bring everything you have and everything you can finish to rehearsal.

It was at this moment that I regretted my self-imposed social isolation. Just a little bit. Because if I took a minute to care about people and their lives, I would know why Evey Paros wanted revenge on Jordan Swansea.

I mean, obviously, they broke up, and maybe he's a shitty guy, but something was missing. A few minutes had already passed from the last text she sent, but I typed out one more.

I can accept that he's a garbage human being. And I even get that breakups suck. But what did he do to you?

She didn't respond right away. In fact, an hour went by before she texted again.

> He took something from me and I want it back.

Not really an answer, but maybe I would find out later. Maybe it was something she would let me in on when she was ready.

Namaste,
Leo

9

Today's Pose: Cobra

I hate snakes.

This is a pose you do on your stomach, hands under your shoulders, pushing up slightly.

Hissing is optional.

A big part of this is probably supposed to be about focusing on the muscles in my body and trying to hold the pose, but instead I stare at the classroom full of people-snakes with their butts clenched.

Dear Journal,

This leads me to the moment where Evey voluntarily sat next to me at pageant rehearsal. Which will be every week until March.

I was sure she was going to ignore me, but that is not what happened.

She sat next to me after my dad dropped me off. Like right next to me in the chair that was touching mine. And we listened to all the little kids practice their Greek poems and get yelled at by adults who thought it was a good idea to give them the swords for their costumes early, rather than when they were supposed to go onstage.

We practice in the big hall off the church. The hall is old and used only for Greek school functions and the March 25 pageant, but it was built to hold wedding receptions.

Note: I would never use this butt-ugly hall for a wedding.

I pretended not to notice that Evey was next to me, but I wasn't good at it. Especially when my eyes were doing that thing where they try to stretch my peripheral vision as far as it'll go. When we stood for the Greek national anthem, I fully expected Evey to be one of those people who don't sing and just move their lips, but I heard her voice. Clear and strong, singing every line perfectly.

I was still in my own little world listening to Evey sing when everyone else sat down. *Vlakas,* my Yia Yia would have hissed at me. *Idiot* was one of her favorite words.

And then my stomach clenched as I realized my Greek teacher was nodding emphatically at me to recite my piece for the Greek school presentation. Little kids got to do little rhymes in a singsongy voice, or they got to stand there and look cute as they repeated after their parents. Mine was some poem about war and bravery that my ancestors would have rolled their eyes at coming from me, but at least I could hide behind the podium and not look up until it was over.

No one expected me to take command of the room with this poem. It was really more of an "Oh, look, he can speak Greek passably—good for him" moment.

When I sat down, I realized Evey wasn't sitting next to me anymore. My phone buzzed.

> Ready to go to work?

She was texting me from the back of the church hall.

We are at rehearsal, I reminded her. Which was probably the stupidest thing I've ever sent to someone else who knows exactly where we are already.

Obviously, she responded.

I wasn't sure how to move the conversation forward. Should I say something else? What would that be? Maybe ask about how she liked the food they laid out? That's something my Yia Yia always did. But that's not something anyone under eighty would say.

We sang the national anthem, she texted. *You already did your speech. No one will know if we're gone.*

She was right. I'd gotten through my memorized poem without stumbling too much, and I always took a seat at the far end of the hall on my own. The rest of the guys my age congregated at the foot of the stage. These are guys who probably should be my friends.

Costa, Nico, Stefano, and Yianni.

They nod in acknowledgment whenever they see me, but they'd formed a clique at a young age, when they were all recruited to be altar boys. I was spared that particular task because I could not quite grasp the concept of swinging incense without hitting myself in the face. I'm actually not *that* uncoordinated, but doing something that requires concentration in front of other people was always a bad idea.

The burn mark from the incense canister is still there at the front of the church. A reminder to all that Leonidas Ermou should not be asked to swing burning ash in a sacred place. Or anywhere, really.

I finally texted Evey back:

> They won't think we're ditching practice together?

She seemed to have been waiting for this response.

> No one would ever think we were doing anything together.

Then—

> Do you have the stuff?

Only Evey Paros could make something as old-ladyish as crocheted blanket squares sound like a drug deal. And I had the stuff I'd been working on in my backpack.

When I got outside the church hall, she flashed the head-lights of her dad's BMW.

"Get in," she said.

I got in.

Revenge is a special kind of angry. You have to earn it. And now I was curious. And there was a duffel bag in the back that had the look of a lumpy body. She seemed to read my mind.

"No one is getting arrested," she said, when I think what she wanted to say was "No one is getting caught."

"My dad is going to wonder where I am."

"So text him. Just tell him you're out with a girl," she said.

Somehow she knew that was something my dad would be okay with.

And sure enough he texted back: *Take your time.*

So I was in a car with Evey on the way to an undisclosed location where I was part of a plot for revenge. The front seat was immaculate except for a stack of magazines with Post-it notes sticking out. I wanted to ask why she'd marked them up, but her expression didn't exactly invite questions.

I imagined my Yia Yia smoking a cigarette in the back-seat. Imagined her shaking her head and looking at Evey in the rearview mirror, Yia Yia's expression one of complete mistrust.

I tried to warn you, agapi mou, she would have said.

We pulled up to a house in an expensive neighborhood with a huge front porch and a long driveway that made a U shape through a weird overpass thing. It wasn't right on the beach, but it was next to the public-access walkway that a lot of rich people like to claim for themselves until the city comes by and removes their private gates because YOU DON'T OWN THE BEACH, MOTHERFUCKER.

The first things I noticed were the cameras.

"They won't see us?" I asked.

"No," she said. "The parents are at some yacht club event, and Jordan has water polo practice until late." I wasn't convinced. "And that camera has been out for months. His dad says it's still a good enough deterrent for thieves. He's the cheapest rich guy alive."

She said it so confidently I just assumed it was all true.

As I write this I realize how stupid that sounds. But they'd only broken up a little while ago. So maybe couples know how to get into each other's houses? Maybe they share garage codes.

I wouldn't really know.

She led me to a side gate, where there was a shed that had a roll-up door like a tiny garage. She rotated the combination lock.

"How do you know the combinations to everything?" I asked.

"He always uses the same one," she said.

But that didn't really answer how she found that out to begin with.

"And I pay attention," she added.

She clicked it open to reveal what can only be described as the most gorgeous mountain bike on the planet.

I was immediately concerned for its safety.

"I never said I was stealing anything," I said.

"Neither did I," said Evey. "No one is stealing anything. And besides, do you really think I'd get caught?"

I must have hesitated, because she got impatient and said, "Look. We are taking pictures to get back at Jordan. And they aren't just going to be pictures of him doing something stupid. This is art. That's why I asked an artist. So calm down and let's go."

I waited until she turned around and then I smiled.

Awkward and definitely blackmailed into taking pictures, but I was an artist, at least. And that was good to hear, even from someone who appeared like she was trying to murder me with her eyes.

She twirled a few more dials on the bike, pulled it out of its resting spot with unnatural strength, then thrust it at me with one hand. I grabbed it quickly and was amazed to discover that it was featherlight. When I seemed shocked by this, Evey made a face.

"Yeah, this bike is over ten grand," she said. I choked, worried again for its safety.

"Don't worry. I won't hurt it," she said, laughing a little as she took off her sweater.

I'm glad that her face was turned away from me when she did that, because I think I stared for a second too long. When she turned back she'd thrown on a Duke University T-shirt and a varsity jacket that was definitely too big for her.

Which of course made it look even better.

I'm not sure what it is about girls wearing men's jackets. But, yeah, it works.

She leaned the bike against the white shed. Her lumpy duffel bag suddenly made sense. Everything started coming out. Battery-powered twinkle lights. Cables. Bungee cords. Extra yarn.

"Your turn," she said, pointing to the bike. When I hesitated, she hissed in Greek, "It's yarn. It is not permanent. Just yarn-bomb it and take the photo."

She leaned back and waited as my focus returned to the bundle of stuff lying on the ground.

My head started to buzz a little and I could feel myself losing control of the situation. I hated being forced into doing something. I hated not being able to take photos on my own terms.

I pulled my stuff out of the bag. Yarn in neon-green colors, granny squares I'd never used for blankets, and finally the letters Evey had asked me to knit. I still didn't quite understand what they were for.

"Start with something like this," Evey said, showing me a photo she'd pulled up of a bike covered in yarn.

"No," I said quietly. "It needs to look like it's lifting off the ground." I'm not sure where I got the idea, but it felt right. Everything arranged itself in a pattern in my head, and I got to work moving the bike so the front wheel lifted about a foot off the ground. Then I covered everything but the handlebars with yarn.

When Evey asked why I was leaving it uncovered, I explained that I wanted the brand to be showing.

She was impressed and started helping me wrap yarn around the spokes and the wheels. It was surprisingly time-consuming, but we worked quickly. I was still afraid that someone was going to show up, even though Evey didn't seem to share my concern at all.

"What else should I hate about this guy?" I asked.

It still felt weird. Creating an art show around humiliating this guy that I didn't know.

"I told you," said Evey, helping me untangle some yarn I was working with. "It's not hate."

"Okay. Well, it's not hate. But it's not just because you're mad he was mean to a kid who had to change schools. And get the rest of your stuff out of the bag, please, so I can see what we're working with." She leaned over and grabbed the stack of SAT prep books.

"More than one kid, actually," she said. "And did you finish knitting that bra? We'll need it for the next photo."

I handed it to her and she laughed. It was neon pink with cups that could have held volleyballs.

"It wasn't just the kid in the porta-potty," Evey said. "He's got a history of meanness that just got less detectable as he got older. Like when he was a kid, he teased Sophie Leon by leaving her secret notes in her desk calling her a porker. And as he got older, he got more creative. Cutting holes in Speedos so water polo teammates couldn't compete. Aggressive fighting under the water that the refs couldn't see.

And when he goes to the beach, he never cleans up his trash. Which might not seem like a big deal, but how much of a douchebag do you have to be to leave trash on the beach?"

She took a deep breath and tossed her hair over her shoulder.

Somewhere in the distance I heard a gate clang shut. I stopped moving.

"It's fine," she said. "It's just Strudel, their German shepherd. He's big but he loves me. We're fine."

"Oh, good," I said. "Glad he loves you. Bet he thinks I'm delicious." Then, under my breath, "Hope he likes Greek."

Evey laughed again, and for a second I forgot I was afraid of this dog that might or might not eat me.

"Now the letters," she said.

I held them out to her and watched as she arranged them on the spokes of the front wheel and, for a second, I paused.

"What?" she asked, and the breeze picked up, lifting the scent of coconut from her hair.

"Nothing," I said. It wasn't nothing; it just wasn't something I would be able to explain because it was the first time I was doing something risky that should elicit a response from my anxiety but I didn't feel it yet. And that weirded me out.

I continued to pull stuff out of my backpack to stop from thinking about it too hard.

She'd told me she wanted me to create thick red letters about six inches in height. They spelled:

L–I–A–R

I flipped on the twinkle lights and hung them over the bike.

"Can you pretend you're sitting on the bike?" I asked.

She was thoughtful for a minute and then walked over to the bike and pretended to sit sidesaddle.

"Wait," I said, getting an idea.

I created a ramp with the stack of books just underneath the front wheel, so if I took the shot from the ground up it was like the bike was taking off into the sky.

She opened the varsity jacket just enough to reveal DUKE on her shirt and then turned her head so her glossy black hair fell in a sheet over her shoulder, obscuring the last name stitched onto the jacket.

She nodded in approval.

"So, you don't care if he knows it's you in these pictures?"

"No," she said.

"Won't he get back at you?" I asked.

"Maybe," she said.

"Well, if he's rich and super-connected, aren't you afraid he'll—"

"What do you care?" she snapped.

"I don't."

"Great. Then just take the picture. Please."

The *please* was added grudgingly, painfully. But she added it because it was almost like she realized at the last second that I wasn't the person she was mad at.

I started taking pictures and didn't say another word.

There's a process to it. I guess everybody is different, but when I take pictures, I pretend nothing exists outside the frame. I snap as many shots as I can in the moment and I keep going.

It was my first time working with an actual living subject who wasn't, like, a plant, so giving Evey direction about where to stand or put her arms or how to tilt her head was different. Good different. It was like creating living art.

And it was strange having Evey look at me like I knew what I was doing.

After a while I brought my camera over to her without saying a word and showed her a few of my favorite shots.

"Perfect," she said.

Evey started to cut the yarn off the bike, but a gate clanged open again and a loud barking filled the air. I quickly unplugged the lights and backed into a wall covered in bougainvillea.

"Don't worry," she said. "I'll calm him down." She walked over to the gate and was about to lower herself to her knees when her eyes shot open wide and she slammed the gate closed, locking us in with the bike.

"That's not Strudel!" she whispered at me. A huge black Doberman had lunged at the gate with its paws and was barking directly into Evey's face. Pretty sure my heart leapt into my throat.

Not only were we on private property, but I could almost feel that dog's massive jaws closing on my throat.

I pulled her away from the gate as footsteps echoed on the driveway.

Evey swore, shoving me into a thick, thorny bush and jumping in on top of me. We rolled as far as we could into the bush and waited.

This was how I was going to die. Mauled to death by a Doberman because I was being blackmailed by a beautiful Greek woman bent on revenge. Despite the crippling fear that we were going to be eaten alive, I couldn't help but notice that Evey was now lying directly on top of me with her cheek pressed into my chest and her hair spread over my face. Which wasn't the most comfortable position. But honestly, not that bad either. If I had to die under a blanket of silky coconut-scented hair, then so be it.

The footsteps got louder, and I started praying under my breath, but the only prayer I could remember was the one that Yia Yia used to say for the evil eye. The dog was barking hysterically, because it could definitely smell us and it definitely knew we weren't supposed to be there.

"Tapatío!" a voice called out.

"Jordan's dad. He must not have gone to the yacht club," she whispered, horrified.

I imagined him discovering us in this bush. Having to explain ourselves. Going to jail.

Then, miraculously, the dog's bark changed, and a soft thud followed by a hiss told us there was a cat nearby.

"Jesus Christ, you dragged me out of the house for a cat?" Jordan's dad swore. "Get inside, you stupid dog!"

We stayed in the bush for about fifteen minutes more, until we felt brave enough to move.

Then we tore the set down and carefully put the bike

back. My hands were shaking as I tried to zip my backpack. Evey reached over and did it for me. More to speed along our exit than out of kindness, though, I think.

We threw our bags over our shoulders and ran back to the car. Neither of us said anything as Evey started the engine and pulled away from Jordan's street.

When we turned out of the neighborhood, I could see Evey's shoulders relax as she tied her hair up at a red light.

"His dad always talked about getting a Doberman when Strudel died. That's a shame. He was a good dog."

"'He was a good dog'?" I whisper-yelled. "We were almost eaten, and *that's* your takeaway from this?"

She rebounded almost immediately. "Look, we got it done. That was the point. Just relax."

"Just relax!"

"Yep. Relax. It's over."

She said it so easily, like all I needed now was a bubble bath and some Ed Sheeran.

She had no idea that my heart would still be racing when I tried to go to sleep tonight. Or that I would replay this scene in my head for weeks.

Relaxing is easy for most people, I thought as I pulled out the camera.

When I looked at the images on the screen, a story unfolded. The word *LIAR* was bold over the neon-green granny squares, and there was Evey riding off on Jordan's bike into the stars, wearing his varsity jacket and, by the looks of it, his T-shirt too.

Evey was almost smiling in a few of the photos, but my

favorite shot was the one that made it look like she was whispering the word *LIAR* as she sat, surrounded by all his stuff now, covered in lurid colors. Her expression was confident and angry. And the word itself could mean anything for an ex-girlfriend, which is why the SAT books she'd stacked underneath the wheel helped the viewer along.

That's what I love about photography. So much of it is about letting the photograph tell a story. We might have set the scene, but there are so many things a good picture can say that words can't. I've never been great at finding the words.

"Did he lie about his test scores?" I asked.

She flashed a grin that I wish I'd been quick enough to catch on film, and then she said, "He lied about a lot of things." And then, sensing that maybe I was slow and didn't understand her meaning, she added, "Yes, he lied about his test scores."

Confidence is interesting. It's a little like magic. Evey walked away from Jordan Swansea's house like having a weird photo shoot outside someone else's bike shed and nearly getting killed by a dog was normal.

She dropped me off at my house without saying goodbye. No "Thanks for taking super-weird pictures, Leo." No "Thanks for coming with me to fulfill my quest for revenge, Leo." Barely any compliments about the photo itself. The one she picked out of the almost hundred images I took.

I was her staff. And it was a little annoying, but I suppose it could be worse.

When I got inside, my dad nodded at me from his chair.

I wasn't used to all this approval, and I opened Yia Yia's bedroom door when I passed it. My dad kept closing the door. It was becoming a weird game between us because closing it made him feel like he could block her out, and opening it was my way of proving to myself that she was still gone. If it was closed, it was like she was on the phone or smoking or doing something that would probably annoy my dad, like watching Greek soap operas.

When I got into my room, I thought about the letters Evey had asked me to crochet.

L–I–A–R

Secrets and lies, agapi mou. They catch up to you, Yia Yia would have said. But she wasn't there.

Namaste,
Leo

10

Today's Pose: Happy Baby

I've gotten used to Annabelle's voice, and the weird thing is how my body reacts when she starts different poses with the same words. Like for happy baby pose she always says, "Now let's give your spine a gentle massage." And I can actually feel my spine straighten up like it knows what's coming.

I lie on my back. Grab my feet. Rock back and forth from side to side holding my toes.

And yeah, I think it actually does make me happy.

Dear Journal,

Evey didn't say a word when she swiped my card in. Nothing about our photo shoot two days ago. She barely raised her eyes to me at all. Even when I dropped a crocheted daisy on her magazines, she only raised her head for half a second to acknowledge my existence.

But that didn't stop me from remembering what it was like to be out with her.

Until the dog showed up, I didn't feel anxious at all when we were together. It was probably because I was taking pictures or getting ready to take pictures. Photography is like another therapy I never really expected to work. The problem is, I can't do it all the time. I can't just focus on the pictures. I have other stuff to do. Like appear human in the sessions with my guidance counselor because I can't knit or crochet around Drake without him asking questions about it.

Do you feel like an old lady when you knit?

Do you make blankets?

Do you make scarves?

Why do you knit?

Who taught you?

And because I can't handle just listening to obnoxious questions anymore, I usually answer as quickly as possible and move on, which is what I was expecting to do yesterday, only something had definitely changed. Drake was different. His hands were sweating, and he kept shaking his head like he was trying to shake off flies.

I ignored him as best I could, but it was distracting. Even by Drake's normal standards. Mr. Thomas was checking his email and hadn't noticed yet, but I could see Drake shifting uncomfortably in his seat, his head moving ever so slightly, but it was almost like he was trying not to.

That was new. He never tried to be inconspicuous.

And today Mr. Thomas was totally oblivious. He was normally up our asses about working together to forge our magical bond of friendship.

"Gentlemen, I'm going to run to the front office. I trust you'll be okay for a second." He didn't even wait for a response. He just went.

Drake was sweating pretty profusely now. His protein drink was sitting on the desk in front of him next to two bananas. Usually he ate quickly, so seeing them sitting there uneaten was definitely weird.

And still I made a valiant effort to ignore him until he started breathing weird.

"Dude, you look sick," I said.

"Yeah," he said, rocking slightly.

"Should you . . . see a nurse?" I asked. If he threw up, I knew I was going to throw up. Watching other people barf always makes me barf without fail. I don't think that's even an anxiety thing. It's just unfortunate.

"Maybe," he said, still rocking.

"Unless you already know what's wrong . . . ?" I prompted.

He turned to me, his lips moving ever so slightly with the effort of keeping himself still. "Adderall," he said. "It's supposed to help me focus, but it's not working like it should."

"Prescription?" I asked.

He seemed irritated.

"Okay," I said. "Is it your first time taking it?"

"Yeah," he said. His skin was pale, and the sweat was starting to pool in his eyebrows like mine did during hot yoga.

"When did you take it?" I asked.

"Last night," he said.

"And . . . are you sure you don't want to go to the nurse?"

"I wasn't supposed to take the first dose last night," he mumbled, "and the nurse hates me."

"Shocker," I said.

His face was so sad and pathetic that I immediately regretted being a dick.

"Sorry," I said, feeling the silence fill the room like a bad smell. "Look," I went on, "do you think you could . . . I dunno . . . nap here?"

I remembered the few times I'd taken medication for anxiety. It had worked, but I had this weird foggy feeling that made me feel unbalanced. Sleep had been the only thing that helped.

Drake stared at me.

"I'll tell Mr. Thomas you're not feeling well."

He couldn't keep his eyes open another second anyway.

"Yeah, okay. Thanks, man."

I nodded, and Drake was snoring like a bull elephant in seconds. He hadn't even taken his backpack off. The new counselor, Ms. Verdant, walked in a minute later and told us that Mr. Thomas had been called into the front office to "defuse a tense situation" and would be back soon.

The air kicked up in the room, and if it hadn't been so cold and uncomfortable, I would have ignored the drop in temperature. I walked over to adjust the thermostat, but nothing happened. The cold air continued to blast us, freezing the whole room.

"I think they're fixing it," said Ms. Verdant, tugging at her cardigan. "The AC never works right in this building."

Drake shivered and his snores warbled.

The counselor didn't notice, but I couldn't stand it.

Cover him up, agapi mou, Yia Yia would have said.

Then I would have said, "But he's the most annoying person on the planet."

He's still cold, she would have said.

And she would have been right.

I took the ugly granny square blanket I was working on and draped it over Drake's shoulders. He stopped shivering, but with his backpack on, he was like some weird humpback creature covered in Muppet fur and mustard-yellow yarn.

Mr. Thomas walked in ten minutes later to relieve the other teacher and glanced at Drake passed out over his desk and then at me with a disgusting smugness on his face. The bell rang and Drake didn't budge.

I picked up my bag.

"He wasn't feeling great. Can you ask him to leave the blanket here and I'll come back to get it later?"

Then I left. Drake was still snoring behind me.

Namaste,
Leo

11

Today's Pose: Tadasana, or Mountain Pose

Basically standing upright like a normal human being.
Nailed it.

Dear Journal,

I feel okay today.

Better than okay. And I think it's because of this class.

People think yoga is a bunch of stretching and lying on a mat and drinking water with pieces of fruit floating in it. And it totally is. But it's also quiet. And with hot yoga, it is about the sweat.

Releasing that much sweat in a confined space and then walking out of the room after a long practice is like pouring out a bucket of yourself, which, honestly, feels terrible while it's happening but feels great when it's done.

It also gives you a lot of time to think. Like about when I saw Drake after I'd given him my blanket. He was standing in the hall near Mr. Thomas's room. He held the blanket out to me.

"Thanks," Drake said, looking down at the blanket.

"You're welcome," I said, and I was surprised that it wasn't awkward.

"So why'd you bail on Fight Club?" he asked as we walked into the room.

"Military self-defense training?" I offered.

"Yeah, whatever. We learn to beat the crap out of other people. Why'd you bail?"

"I dunno."

Mr. Thomas wasn't there yet, so we just took our usual seats in the desks facing each other.

"C'mon. Yeah you do," Drake said.

"It's not my thing."

"It's not that bad," he said. "And actually you could probably learn something. It's useful."

"I was out at the warriors' chant," I said.

He considered this. "Okay, that's fair. But you still could have learned something. There are plenty of assholes out there ready to knock you the fuck out."

"There's an asshole here who did," I said. But now I was laughing.

"You know what I mean," Drake said, waving off my *asshole* comment and laughing too.

"I'm just not that kind of guy," I said, shrugging.

"What kind of guy are you?"

"The kind who doesn't want to talk about fighting."

"We are stuck here for an hour. Do you really think you can just knit the whole time without talking? WHAT. KIND. OF. GUY. ARE. YOU?"

Actually I was sorta hoping I *could* knit the whole time without talking.

Then Mr. Thomas dropped his water bottle, and I could tell he was really pissed at himself for interrupting what he probably thought was a breakthrough moment, when he was trying to sneak in quietly.

What Drake said felt like something a personal trainer might say to motivate someone to answer a deeply personal question and help them reveal their inner strength.

I wasn't biting.

"Look," said Drake. "You can be the kind of guy who doesn't want to learn to fight because you don't like the other guys who fight OR you can learn anyway because it's something good to know. I've been taking martial arts my whole life."

"Then why are you taking the class?"

"The guy who teaches it is Brad Hardwick. He's my stepdad."

"Oh."

"He's not as stupid as his name sounds. So what kind of guy are you?"

I rolled my eyes hard.

Just answer him, agapi mou, Yia Yia would have said.

"Are you just not a fan of self-defense?" Drake asked, and there was something almost sympathetic about the way he cocked his head to one side and raised an eyebrow. Like he was actually trying to help.

"I'm not a fan of people," I blurted out.

I immediately regretted saying it, but Drake laughed long and hard and then looked at me with a fake seriousness and said, "You know you're people, right?"

"I guess." God, I sounded pathetic.

"There's people in yoga too," Drake offered.

"It's quiet," I said. "And nobody wants to hit me."

I could tell Drake wanted to say something along the lines of "Plenty of people want to hit you, Leo." But he held back, which was surprising.

"Plus, I don't really have a choice. I sort of promised I'd help Evey Paros with something because she switched me out of that self-defense class."

"Really?" Drake asked with interest. "What?"

"I can't tell you."

And for some reason Drake blew this off like it was nothing.

"Evey has been best friends with my girlfriend, Jen, since they both quit Girl Scouts together. She's all right. And now I can tell her we're friends."

"Are we friends?" I asked as people started filling up the hallway again before class.

"Dude, you knit me a blanket, so . . . don't make this weird."

I tried to explain that I didn't, in fact, knit him a blanket, but the bell rang and Drake was laughing too much to hear me anyway.

So now I think we might be friends.

Namaste,
Leo

12

Today's Pose: Bow

Lie on your stomach and reach back to grab your ankles.
    Rock.
    Lose your balance and fall over sideways but try to land gracefully.
    Fail miserably with a loud thud.
    Pretend no one looks over.

Dear Journal,

Drake has made it his mission in life to teach me to fight. And I regret ever giving him my phone number.

    Now I get a series of motivational texts every day.

Today you are a new man.

That's a lie. You're exactly
the same. Which is why
you need to stay hydrated
and not eat garbage.

But it's a new day. Let's
crush it. You are a warrior.

That's what Drake told me to say to myself in the mirror.

I told him he was full of shit, but I did show up before yoga like he asked. I told Dad I was meeting someone before class, and he accepted it without question.

Drake started by trying to teach me how to throw a punch.

"Has it occurred to you that this is weird?" I asked.

Drake stared at me and cocked his head.

"Because you punched me in the face. You are the reason I am here at all. And now you are the one teaching me how to punch someone else in the face?"

I stared at him for a while, watching him think. He was already tired from lifting, so it looked like hard work.

"Can you shut up, please?" he said. "You're standing wrong and you're basically getting destroyed by anyone who wants to attack you at this point."

I don't actually think there is going to be an immediate

need to use these self-defense skills, but I fixed my stance anyway.

Drake mostly ignores the stuff he doesn't want to talk about. Like, he probably doesn't want to think about the test results he's got crammed in his backpack. He's failing algebra and even though he acts like it doesn't bother him, nobody slams a math book in their backpack like that unless it's done them wrong.

When he finished correcting me, we still had a few minutes until I had to change for yoga, so I pulled out some pink fluffy yarn I'd been using for a couple of matching baby hats.

Drake's expression demanded an explanation, but then he said, "Dude, are you pregnant?"

"I have an Etsy store for my yarn stuff," I said.

I started to explain Etsy to Drake. When I got to the part about having my own store, he interrupted.

"So what's your store called?" he asked. I showed him the website, where my store owner account was highlighted.

He read the store name out loud. *"Hooked?"*

"Yeah," I told him. "It's for the crochet hook. Get it?"

He didn't. But he nodded.

"And you sell this stuff online?" he asked.

"Yeah, so it's a website where individual craftspeople can sell handmade—"

"Got it." Drake cut me off midsentence because he was done pretending to be interested. "There's a couple of teams who could use some stuff. Scarves. Beanies. How fast can you knit?"

"Pretty fast," I told him.

So at lunch, instead of letting me eat by the benches near my locker, Drake dragged me over to his basketball teammates, who wanted some beanies. That's when he introduced me to Jen, who walked over with some friends from her track team, who wanted to know if I could crochet some wristbands. They were all wearing their uniforms already for their meet after school.

"Heard a lot about you from Evey," she said, and for a second I wondered if she knew about the photographs, until she said, "But she won't say what you guys are actually up to together."

Jen's long dark brown hair was pulled back in a ponytail. She was wearing her track uniform already, just like the rest of her team. Her last name, CISNEROS, was emblazoned on her back.

Evey was mysteriously absent from the quad, and when I looked around for her, Jen seemed to read my mind.

"Evey usually avoids the quad at lunch," she said, jutting her chin toward a table nearby with Jordan's circle, and the cheerleader sitting on his lap.

For the rest of the lunch period athletes walked up and placed orders.

"I didn't realize there was such a high demand for old-lady stuff," said Drake. "I mean beanies, yeah. But that guy just ordered a baby hat for his sister's kid."

"People like handmade stuff," I said, smiling.

Then a weird thing happened.

Jordan came over and placed an order too.

It's strange to think Jordan goes to my school. It feels implausible that someone so good-looking and rich could be in the same place as the rest of us. So when I say he goes to my school, I mean he basically just sometimes occupies the same space I do in various rooms we both need to be in. To say that he and I go to the same school is to say that we are also on the same planet. The important thing to remember is that he is rich and that I have seen him. Tall, with shiny brown hair that has an effortlessly surferlike quality about it. Blue eyes. He's basically the deluxe package to the hot-guy starter kit.

And on top of all that, he is on the water polo team. While a lot of kids have to sell candy or cookie dough or their organs to pay for some weird-ass "Spirit Pack" that contains all the clothes they'll need to compete, he's one of the kids who just buys it.

"Hey," he said. "I heard you knit. I'm looking for something for the team. Think you can do twelve light blue beanies by next week? Please?"

"That's a lo—" I started to say, but before I could complete the rest of the sentence, he pulled out a wad of cash like they do in the movies and handed it all to me.

"I know it's last-minute. Thanks, man. I appreciate it!" He slapped me on the arm in a very bro-y way. Like he's already trained for his future life in a frat house and politics with other equally attractive, rich white guys.

He'd paid me three times my usual rate. He didn't wait for me to say whether I'd be able to do it. He just went back to his adoring crowd, and the cheerleader took her spot on his lap again.

Jen watched all this happen with a strange look on her face.

That was the annoying thing about Jordan. Everything he said out loud was fine. *Please. Thanks. Smile.* On paper he was perfect. But there was something about him that made me uncomfortable. Like you knew he was lying to your face but you couldn't prove it.

I tried to explain it to Drake at the end of the period.

"He's really good at doing what he wants and not getting caught," Drake said.

"What does he do?" I asked.

I thought about Evey and the photos and everything the photos said without actually saying it.

Drake hesitated.

"It's nothing you could prove. Like I said, he's really good at just making things happen. He's almost perfect. But only *almost,* because being perfect would be too much of a giveaway, you know?" Drake said seriously. "I told Evey to be careful with him when they started dating, but she didn't listen. She really liked being popular, and I think she regrets that now," he added, sitting on the table with his giant feet on the bench.

"But you're popular," I blurted out. And Drake actually laughed while Jen rolled her eyes.

"No," he said. "I'm loud, and people know who I am. But popular takes work. It's about . . ." Drake struggled to find the words, but Jen chimed in.

"It's about people knowing who you are and thinking good things about you because of what other people say about you. Not because they know you. And it's about feeling powerful. Evey liked that." Then she stopped talking as Jordan's friends laughed nearby, and she scowled.

I thought about this on the mat while Annabelle held me in place for the third time for bow pose. It is really weird being handed your own foot to hold, but maybe there's a lesson there about flexibility. She holds me in place, and I rock back and forth and listen to my back crack and think about what it means to be popular.

I'd never really thought about being popular, because popular means people. And people are not my thing. Or at least, people weren't my thing.

But I didn't mind being around Drake and Jen at lunch. I know it was mostly just being surrounded by people who wanted me to knit stuff for them, but there was something kinda peaceful about being with them and not feeling weird about it. Like being part of a stream. Going with the current. And not like I was doing stuff just because everyone else was doing it, but because I felt connected to something.

Which is remarkably Zen of me.

Still, I missed Evey at lunch and wondered where she'd been. She wasn't at the front desk just now either,

110

but I dropped a crocheted violet on her growing stack of magazines.

I wondered when I'd finally get a text from her about my gifts.

It came later.

> Why do you keep leaving me yarn flowers?

> Because I'm trying to be nice.

> Why?

> I don't know, actually. This is the bullshit part where I should make a little speech about kindness changing people. Because you haven't actually been nice and you don't exactly deserve flowers.

I hit Send, and I didn't regret it. It's easier to be honest via text than it is in person. There are no eyes to face. No awkward silences. I can just hit Send and pretend it didn't go anywhere if I want. But then she texted back and it confirmed that it had, in fact, reached its recipient.

> Then you should probably only make people what they deserve.

Impossible in this case.

I believe in you.

I sat back and stared at the text for a while. Then I pulled out some brown yarn.

Namaste,
Leo

13

Today's Pose: Upward Dog

This is a back-bending yoga pose that is supposed to strengthen the spine, torso, and arms.

You lie on your stomach with your palms on the floor by your hips, then push yourself all the way up on your palms.

It's one of those poses that actually makes me feel like the thing it's named after, because everyone really does look like a dog stretching in the sun.

But if there's a pose where you drag your butt across the floor, I'm out.

Dear Journal,

Drake came to my house before yoga yesterday. Dad wasn't home yet, so it gave Drake the opportunity to look through our fridge while I was changing. I heard some noise coming from the kitchen, but wasn't sure what he was doing until I walked in and saw a garbage bag on the floor.

He was typing something on his phone when I walked in. Then my phone buzzed.

> If I see you with another microwave burrito I am going to set all your yarn on fire. I brought you a salad for lunch tomorrow. Your stomach might not process it because it isn't plastic. You're welcome.

> PS I only threw out the packages that are filled with massive amounts of preservatives. I left a few Lean Cuisines, but don't buy that crap anymore.

I didn't bother to tell him it was weird to text me from four feet away. Then he sent his motivational text of the day.

> The dung beetle has to roll a pile of shit up a hill to feed his family before it dries out in the hot sun.

Next time you criticize my kale
smoothie I would like you to
consider dung beetle babies
waiting for Dad to get home
with actual shit for dinner.

Also never give up.

I couldn't if I tried.

And I've actually tried giving up.

In class everyone has a role. Mine is to do nothing.

Carol is easily the most balanced human on the planet. Damaris does yoga with a really intense look on her face, like she's mad she has to relax. Tiffany, Bri, and Catherine, who are all going to different colleges next year, take turns crying about how much they're going to miss each other in the fall. Stephanie ends every single class with a loud OMMMMMMM that everyone joins in on, but otherwise she makes no noise whatsoever. And Annabelle leads us all with the grace of a gazelle, but the minute the class is over, you can see her face fall, like wherever she's going next is loud and chaotic and she's storing up all the quiet for later.

I guess I don't actually do nothing. It just seems that way because everyone else does what they're supposed to.

Nicole and Tara are impossibly good at every pose they do, and instead of being jerks about it, they spend a lot of time helping me. Last class Nicole fixed my hand placement and Tara fixed my feet and both of them hovered over me until my vinyasa flow was less slothlike. I think Annabelle might have asked everyone to take turns with me. It's probably exhausting to be the only person dealing with the slow learner in the room.

Tiffany, Bri, and Catherine are committed to teaching me how to do a headstand. But I've come perilously close to snapping my own neck a few times during class. Tiffany teaches me how to cradle my own head. Bri holds my waist to help me hinge upward. And Catherine . . . Well, I accidentally kicked her in the forehead, causing a minor panic while all of them discussed the huge red welt and whether it would be visible for cheerleading photos at the beach. Understandably, Catherine hasn't helped much since.

Damaris. It's true that she definitely looks more intense than everyone else in the class, but I think that's just how she focuses. She looks at yoga as an exercise, which is serious business. Like taking your medicine. Not something to be done lightly. She is also strictly nontouch when correcting me. She whispers what I'm doing wrong, then waits until I move properly into position.

Yesterday after I left yoga, Evey sent me a text:

9:00 tonight. I'll pick you up.

I didn't get any other information, and she hadn't asked me to make anything specific, so I wasn't really sure what to expect.

But then Drake sent me a text about ten minutes later.

Hey looks like I'll see
you tonight. Don't panic.
You're people too.

That actually made me feel a little better, but I was confused. Had Evey told Drake and Jen about what we were doing and they were coming with us?

I'm never really sure what to expect with Evey. She hadn't even texted me yet with any stuff for the next photo shoot. Which was fine, especially with all the new orders I was doing at school for kids who suddenly knew my name.

Cool. But definitely weird.

I told my dad I was going out, and he seemed fine with it. The fridge had a few essentials that Drake had left during his most recent inspection. Some vegetables, salad, and a few cold cuts for sandwiches. It really did look like our fridge was trying to be normal and failing miserably, so I refilled my water bottle and closed the door.

A sad pot of rice my dad had given up on was sitting on the counter. He was eating some weird takeout from a Greek place pretending to be authentic, so I ate a kebab and some pita with tzatziki. We'd gotten used to eating the same food in the same place without speaking. I stood over the sink while food fell from my mouth, and he sat in his chair in front of the TV while pieces of food fell onto his lap.

I'd already given Jordan his order of beanies on Monday. I'd finished all of them over the weekend, and he appraised me, mildly impressed, but there was also a definite look of judgment for the pathetic knitter.

Why does everyone insist that being a knitter is pathetic? Or I guess being alone is pathetic.

There's a difference between being alone and being lonely.

Lonely is sad, but alone can be liberating. It's possible to be one and not the other. You can be lonely in a crowd of people. And you can be happily alone.

Alone can mean good things like eating cereal in your underwear or leaving a place exactly when you want to. It can be not worrying about saving ice cream for anyone.

Fun fact: there has been a single Snickers Ice Cream Bar in our freezer since Yia Yia died. Dad and I both like them, but neither of us wanted to eat the last one. I thought maybe Dad didn't notice, but then I witnessed him opening the freezer, picking up the ice cream package, and putting it back. He didn't want to eat the last one either.

I told Drake about that during our next training session and he looked stricken.

"So there's ice cream sitting in your freezer that you both want, and instead of buying another box, like regular human people, you stare at it?"

It's hard to explain to someone like Drake that talking is the problem. Drake never would have let it get to a point where someone close to him didn't know *exactly* what he was thinking when he was thinking it. He has this prevailing need to be understood, which usually results in TMI.

Like, I don't need to know when he has to poop. Or when the elastic on his underwear is too tight. Or when he forgets deodorant.

That last one is obvious anyway. And he talks a lot about being concerned about his grades.

"It's hard dating a math genius," he said. "I'd be jealous if AP Calc was a dude. Actually I'm already a little jealous. She looks at her textbook the way other people look at puppies."

So I ask the obvious question: "Why don't you have your supersmart girlfriend tutor you?"

"It's complicated."

"What?"

"She's distracting. So I suggested finding a less hot tutor and she lost it. Like I was cheating on her with math. And I still don't understand the fight we had, man."

"Why don't you just do a video chat? Not of each other," I said quickly when he raised his eyebrows. "You show your screens. That way she can teach you, and you don't have to look at her."

He thought about it. "Can I tell her it was my idea?"

"Sure," I said, pulling a Coke out of my bag.

"Thanks, man," said Drake. "I appreciate it."

Then he reached over, grabbed my Coke, and threw it into the recycle bin.

"Saving you from yourself," he said. "If you want to punch me, let's use that to fix your uppercut. Cuz right now it sucks." He handed me my water bottle, and I stared longingly at the recycle bin for a while before getting up to work on my uppercut. Because he was right. I sorta did want to punch him.

I finished my training with Drake. Went to yoga. And

then at 9:00 p.m. Evey was waiting for me by the curb with the engine running.

"Where are we going?" I asked.

She didn't answer. Her hair was down in loose waves around her face, and her mouth was twisted into a slight frown. She was looking at my clothes like they were a dead animal I was about to bring into the car. I was wearing a white T-shirt and jeans. Nothing offensive about that. Or so I thought as I reached for the passenger door handle. She shook her head at me.

"Go in the backseat and put these on," she said.

She handed me a stack of clothes.

"How did you know my clothes were going to be unacceptable?" I asked.

"Because I have seen you."

"Ouch. What's wrong with T-shirts and jeans?" I asked.

"Nothing when they're your size. But you're wearing clothes that are too big for you. Just put those on, please."

There were dark jeans and a super-soft blue T-shirt. When I slid into the backseat to change, there was another stack of magazines, this time filled with white sheets of typed paper.

"Is there a reason I have to change to take photos at an undisclosed location?" I asked, looking at the magazines.

"We're not doing that tonight," she answered.

I guess I should have been used to being confused. But I was under the impression that I only existed to her when she needed me to take photos.

"We're not?"

"No, we're going to a party."

My stomach clenched, but at least I wouldn't have to worry about explaining anything to my dad.

There are a few benefits to having a dad who is emotionally unavailable. Aside from the sparkling conversation and the warm, fuzzy feelings of acceptance and love, there is the fact that he respects my privacy. And doesn't freak out if I come home late.

Which I never do, but he wouldn't if I did. And it's nice to know I have that option.

But parties are torture. They have been torture my entire life. I don't think I've ever enjoyed one before, which sounds pretty pathetic, but that doesn't mean I haven't enjoyed other stuff. It's just that parties are super . . . people-y. And people mostly suck.

"Uh. Why?"

"What does it matter to you?" she asked. "Did you have other plans?"

"Maybe I don't want to go to a party," I told her. I think there was a piñata at the last one I went to. I ate two pieces of cake and vomited in the bouncy castle. I haven't been to a party since.

Yia Yia would have said, *A party won't kill you, agapi mou.* She was probably right.

"Look," I said. "I don't do parties. They kinda make me . . ." I didn't finish the sentence. And to my surprise Evey's face actually softened a little.

"We're just making an appearance." Which sounded like a nice way of saying that I was going whether I wanted to or not.

"Could you, like, look away?"

She smirked and turned her gaze away from the rearview mirror. As I pulled on the pants I could feel the material hug my butt.

"Uh. I don't know if these are going to fit," I said.

"They'll fit," she said. "And these are soft. You'll like them. Trust me."

They fit. They were soft. And I did like them.

I grumbled a little bit because she was right and I could tell she was smiling.

"Hurry up so we can go," she said.

"Where'd you get these clothes?" I asked.

"The store," she said evasively. "Come back up front."

I slid out of the backseat and opened the front door and was momentarily distracted by Evey's dress, which was just low enough to see where her necklace dipped between her breasts, and I looked away but not quickly enough as I got into the passenger seat.

Because I'm not a monk.

Before I could say anything stupid she leaned forward and ran her fingers through my hair and fixed the tag on my shirt (which, by the smell of it, was brand-new).

All the places where her fingers touched me felt hot, and I tried not to look at her as she leaned back into her seat to drive, even though I was still thinking about how close she'd just been. Like when we'd both been in that bush at Jordan's.

"Okay," she said, appraising me. "Let's go." She turned on the car and we pulled out onto the main street.

Ten minutes later we were there. Though I wasn't really sure where *there* was.

It was a big house with a gated courtyard and a large terra-cotta pot fountain out front surrounded by succulents. There was a steady flow of people moving through the front door, but the front yard was oddly quiet.

"Not a big party, then," I said hopefully.

"The place is bigger on the inside," she said.

"Like the Tardis," I muttered.

"Like what?"

"Never mind."

She killed the engine and turned to me, examining the effects of my wardrobe change with interest.

"Okay," she said, appraising me again. "Let's go."

A sudden feeling of panic rose inside me. I could feel my intestines tightening like a thousand little fleshy knots, but then I thought of my dad's call to Greece the other day and the looming threat of sending me to live with my cousins so they can teach me how to be a man.

I grabbed my leather camera satchel and put it around my neck.

"You can't bring that in."

"I'm not leaving it in the car."

She stared at me and I wondered how she was going to

handle this moment. She adjusted the strap so it hung at my side.

"Fine," she said. "Here are the rules."

"Rules?" I asked.

"Yeah," she said. "We don't have to stay long. Like I said, we're just making an appearance. Be the strong, silent type. Less is more. Choose your words carefully."

"Because I'll say something stupid and embarrass you?" I said acidly.

"Because I want to get in and out as quickly as possible. Are you in or not?"

"Fine," I said.

I thought about asking her whose house this was or why we were here if the intention was to leave almost immediately, but since all I wanted to do was leave immediately, I kept my mouth shut.

I followed her up the walkway, where we were greeted by three other girls holding red cups, who shrieked when we arrived. Evey waved at them but kept moving.

"Not going to introduce me?" I asked.

I was joking, but she said, "They're already drunk. They won't remember."

We walked inside and Evey had been right. The house was a huge place that opened up into a big backyard with a deck and a pool. Most people were holding red cups and sitting on the couches that wrapped all the way around the family room, but there were a few guys in the pool riding what looked like inflatable golden swans. It would have probably been a nice place, but people were already trashing it.

Evey leaned toward me and said, "This house belongs to one of Jordan's friends. His parents are out of town."

"So is Jordan coming?" I asked.

She didn't say anything.

Couples were basically sitting all over each other. It was clear that couches from other rooms had been moved downstairs. There were chips ground into the carpet and empty bottles covering all the tables. Everyone who wasn't sitting was holding a red cup. The smell of beer, which seemed to have soaked into the carpet, made my stomach turn.

Evey led me to an empty spot on one of the couches. The only empty spot. I perched on the arm of the chair next to her because that was the only place that made sense. And I was like a strange bird man with a camera . . . or a super-awkward bodyguard.

"Hi, Leo," said Jen. She always seemed to appear out of nowhere.

She appraised me and noticed the small leather bag.

"Camera?" she asked.

Evey gave her a warning look, but Jen just smiled. Then a group of girls who I recognized from AP US History spotted Evey from across the room and pulled her up off the couch.

"Evey, they made jungle juice!" one of them shrieked.

Evey mouthed, "I'll be right back," and then the crowd swallowed her, leaving me alone with Jen and the fifty other people in the room.

"You look hot," Jen said finally.

I looked at her and laughed.

"Don't let Drake hear you say that," I said.

"He's fine." She laughed. "As long as I tell him he's pretty too."

No one had ever said that to me before, and her straight-forwardness was disarming. She was holding an empty red cup, and since she didn't seem drunk, I wondered if she was just holding it because everyone else was. That seemed like a good plan. I grabbed one off the floor and felt instantly better to be holding a prop.

"I mean that could be why she brought you here," she said, thinking it over. "Don't look at me like that," she added while I laughed. "You have everything. The dark, mysterious eyes. You're taller than she is. And you're not a jerk."

I didn't know what to say to that.

"How do you know I'm not a jerk?"

"I can tell," Jen said.

There was no way Evey had brought me as arm candy, but I caught a glimpse of myself in the glass table and was surprised that I did look a little different. Maybe not hot. But not bad.

I glanced around the room and frowned a little.

"You're not really into this, are you?" asked Jen.

"Not really my thing, no," I said.

"Then why'd you come?" Jen asked.

I was about to say "Because Evey asked." But she hadn't.

She'd just told me to come. And for some reason I'd come along, so I just shrugged instead.

"Evey has been my best friend since we were little. And I love her like a sister, but her judgment has been skewed recently."

I tilted my head because I wanted her to keep going.

"She didn't want to come alone. That's for sure. But it doesn't hurt that you're hot. Also, can I see your camera?"

I hesitated.

"I'll be careful," she promised. She held it up to her eye and began snapping pictures. "Oh wow, it's like an actual camera with a click and everything," she said.

God help me, I thought.

Evey came back through a door leading to the kitchen, looking harassed.

"What have you two been talking about?" she asked.

"Nothing," said Jen. "Smile!"

She pointed the camera at the two of us and Evey went to put up her hand, and I couldn't help it. I reached out and caught it gently and whispered, "Would it really be so terrible to be caught on film with me?"

I said it in Greek, and something about the moment seemed to catch her off guard. The closeness, I think. Her nose was inches from mine when I leaned in, and she opened her eyes wider in amusement and a smirk crossed her face as Jen snapped the photo. I heard the click and let go of her fingertips, a little surprised by her reaction. Jen watched us with interest and handed the camera back to me.

Then some guys I recognized as Drake's basketball team-mates appeared in the living room with a funnel and a keg and everything got louder. Someone turned the volume on the music all the way up, and the guys holding the keg started shouting.

More people crowded into the room and I saw Evey and Jen both lean back to watch with an almost lazy expression on their faces, but something in me started to feel off, so I told them I was going to find a bathroom.

Sound is a huge thing for me. Even on days when I feel in control and don't have any anxiety attacks, the wrong noise can really destroy my focus. Raised voices. Music. Even the footsteps on the ground and the sound of stuff moving around in the kitchen seemed like a cheese grater to my brain.

When I was really small I craved quiet. My cousins couldn't figure out why I got so antsy at family gatherings. Why I flinched whenever Demetri screamed, because my cousin doesn't exactly have volume control. My entire Greek family doesn't have volume control.

And there I was in a room full of people and I was going to be the guy who blew chunks by the keg.

No, I'm not, I thought.

But it was happening. I could feel it. It's that moment when your stomach starts to churn in that gross rhythmic way that sends chills up your spine because you know you're about to release the Kraken.

The bile rose up from my stomach to my throat as I searched for a bathroom.

But I was blocked everywhere I turned.

Outside, I thought. *I just have to get outside.*

But even the wide-open doors to the pool were crowded with people. I moved through them, keeping my hand over my mouth, forcing my way past slow-moving drunk people. Somewhere ahead there might be air and quiet and freedom, but I was blocked again by another sweaty couple making out.

Finally I spotted access to the outside just off the kitchen and vomited spectacularly into some shrubs while a few guys observed me casually during their jousting match astride the inflatable golden swans.

"Good sir!" said one of the swan riders. "Dost thou vomit upon my mother's geraniums?" The other swan rider laughed.

Then I felt a hand on my shoulder and heard a familiar voice. "Whoa, dude. How much did you have?"

It was Drake.

"Not drunk," I said, still feeling a little dizzy. "It's the noise, I think."

It wasn't like when I had to explain Etsy to him. He got it right away.

"This is actually the best place to have a panic attack," Drake whisper-shouted. "Everyone will just think you drank too much."

I swayed a little.

"Perfect," he said. "Just like that."

He was right. It was lucky that it happened here in a place where I could blame alcohol, which is so much easier than blaming anxiety. That's bizarre, though, right? I can't blame a natural reaction in my brain, but I can blame a recreational liquid I choose to drink and that's socially acceptable?

"Evey brought you, right?" Drake shouted over the music as we walked back inside.

I didn't feel entirely safe opening my mouth again, but then I spotted Evey still sitting on the couch where I'd left her.

"You okay now?" he asked. "Here. Hold this." He handed me a half-full red cup.

"No thanks," I said. "That smells awful."

"It's not worse than your puke breath, dude. Just swish and spit."

I hesitated, then swished what I'm pretty sure was whiskey in my mouth, then spit it into a potted plant to my right.

"Cool," he said, clapping me on the back. "I'll meet you over there," he added, gesturing toward Jen.

"Let's go," Evey said, grabbing my arm. She was looking over her shoulder.

"Leaving?" Jen asked. She and Evey had a silent conversation about it and Jen indicated a room toward the back of the house.

"You don't have to leave," Jen said.

"I just wanted to make an appearance," Evey told her.

"You should probably do more than that," said Jen, and out of the corner of my eye I saw a guy walk through the door holding a girl's hand, but before I could get a good look at either of them, Evey grabbed my face and was kissing me. Not urgently. Not drunkenly. Gently and with purpose.

I was profoundly aware of the fact that I had just rinsed puke out of my mouth with whiskey, but if she thought I was gross, she didn't say it.

And I kissed her back.

She slid her hands into my back pocket and I leaned into a kiss I didn't really know I wanted until it happened.

When we broke apart she smiled at me, but then I saw her eyes flicker ever so slightly toward Jordan, who had definitely noticed us through the crowd of people.

And my stomach dropped because it was more than being dressed up as a decoy.

I'd just gotten my first kiss, and it hadn't even been real. I was a prop, and I had let it happen.

"Let's go," she said again, and because I was completely outside my comfort zone, I barely registered the walk back to the car.

I was hurt, but it felt like I wasn't allowed to be.

She didn't put on the music in the car, which was nice because my insides were just starting to untangle. And then I stupidly decided to make conversation.

"Are you still going to pretend you don't know me at the gym?"

"Am I what?" she said.

It was a red flag. A dangerous tone. I should have known better, but I kept going.

"Every time I hand you my card to swipe me in to class, you barely look up," I said.

"And?"

"Well, I mean. You could smile or something."

It was the absolute wrong thing to say.

"I guess I *could*," said Evey, her tone suggesting that I had made a grave error in judgment. "Is there anything else I should do for you? In addition to the smiling, of course," she asked.

"That's not what I meant—" I started to say.

"If I wanted your opinion on how I should act, I would have asked for it," she said in Greek.

It reminded me how easily the language flew out of her. The way a language can if both parents speak it at home. She hurled the words at me effortlessly, and that's when I got angry.

"Fair enough, but don't kiss me unless you mean it. That was a shitty thing to do."

Her eyes opened wide at my response in Greek, and there was silence in the car again.

I didn't say it felt weird to be blackmailed into doing something artistic that I might have wanted to do anyway. And I didn't say she could have just asked and I would have helped. I didn't say any of those things, because now I felt used. Actually used. The photography was one thing, but a kiss to make someone jealous. That was a new low.

She didn't say anything and the silence grew, filling the car like water until I thought it was going to drown us.

She pulled up in front of my house, and I got out the second we stopped moving, without looking back.

I tried to process what had just happened, but I couldn't wrap my head around the whole situation.

Drake said Evey was all right. And Jen said Evey was her best friend, which was also weird, because Jen seemed nice. Based on my own experience with Evey Paros, she was a manipulative, revenge-seeking siren who dragged me to a party so she wouldn't show up alone and kissed me in front of her ex-boyfriend to prove she was fine after what appeared to be a not-great breakup.

I got back to my room and threw myself on my bed. My little star projector still sat on my shelf, but I was not going to turn it on. (1) Because it probably didn't work anymore and (2) because I was not going to sit here and feel sorry for myself.

I chose to go to that party. I could have said no thanks, but I went because she wanted me to and I liked that she wanted me there.

My camera strap was still around my neck, so I took it off and threw it on the end of my bed. Then I remembered Jen's pictures and I sat up. My camera was digital, but it still made the old-fashioned click noise like a camera with film, but I guess even that's kind of a novelty when most people take pictures on their phones.

I opened the lens and saw the picture that Jen had snapped when I'd leaned in toward Evey to ask her if it was really so terrible to take a picture with me. I was holding

Evey's fingertips and pulling her hand away from her face. I'd just whispered to her, and her mouth had just started to turn up into a smile.

It was before the fake kiss, but this moment was real. Her smile was real and so was mine.

Then my phone buzzed.

Hey.

Hey.

I'm sorry, Leo. I'm sorry I kissed you.

You did it just to make him jealous?

I think I did it to prove that I'm fine. And not in love with him. I don't know. It was stupid. And I'm sorry.

You might not be in love with him. But you're not fine if you're willing to kiss someone just to prove a point.

Texting really does make you braver. It's like a glorious mask enabling complete honesty. A few seconds passed before she responded.

You're right.

And also I don't dress that badly. But these jeans really DO make my ass look incredible.

Let's not get carried away.

Like, I want me right now.

Wow.

Anyway, I'm sorry.
Are we okay?

Well, I won't be knitting you flowers anytime soon.

I suppose I deserve that.

Then I went to sleep.

Just now before class when I handed her my gym card, she lifted her eyes to me. I wanted to look away, but I didn't.

"Leo," she said, handing me back my card.

I dropped something on her keyboard and walked to class.

There was a message on my phone when I finished yoga.

Did you seriously knit me a poop?

I did. Because you told me to knit you what you deserve.

You're really not this honest in person.

Because you're a little scary.

But you still made me an actual poop made of yarn. You think that'll help the curse?

No. But I thought it might make you laugh.

It did . . .

Thanks.

Namaste,
Leo

14

Dear Journal,

It was weird waking up after the party and the kiss and the weird aftermath of making up with someone completely via text. Especially when that someone was technically still blackmailing me.

But it was Saturday, and I was feeling oddly at peace with the world.

Then my phone buzzed with a text from Evey.

> Bring the giant bra tonight. All
> the neon colors you have and
> the other crocheted letters.

> Good morning. And how are you? That's how you talk to people nicely.

> You knit me a poo.

> With my very own hands.

> Good morning. And how are you?

> Oh you know. Blackmailed. Confused. Hungry.

> Rough life. Bring the giant bra tonight. And all the other old-lady crap you have.

> Bring the poo.

> I'm not bringing the poo.

I got up and walked into the kitchen, where my dad was having breakfast.

"It's supposed to rain later. Bring an umbrella," he said.

"Okay."

"Do you need a ride to the gym tonight?"

"I think Drake is coming to get me."

I think Dad knows we train together. I mean, I'm sure he does. I've mentioned it, but he doesn't ask for details, which is a relief. Sometimes the lack of conversation is convenient.

We have one car, and it would be slightly inconvenient for Dad if the car were parked outside the gym, but the real reason he usually has to drive me is because I can't. Well, I probably can, but I've never really tried to drive. After that one failed attempt at driver's ed, I never went back.

Yia Yia had never pushed me to learn because she never got her license either.

She had one driving lesson in Greece when she was a girl, and apparently she killed a goat. A little white one.

She never got behind the wheel again.

So she never pushed me, which was nice.

Everyone around me is stoked to get their license, and I can't even fake enthusiasm. When I explained this to Drake, he sent me a confused-face emoji, but he rebounded pretty quickly.

Whatever, I'll pick you up.

It's okay. You don't have to do that.

Do you have epic knitting plans today?

I imagined his obnoxious grin.

Drop whatever gross food you're secretly eating.

I'll be there in twenty. Jen and Evey will meet us there later.

Why?

Because Jen is my girlfriend and she told Evey we were training. So now they're both coming.

I agreed like ten seconds ago.

Keep up, Leo.

Also, today you are going to fuck up that plastic dummy. Like seriously, fuck him up.

Then we're getting quinoa at mother's market. Game plan.

• • •

"Heading out," I called to Dad, but Drake had already raced up the driveway before I could stop him and asked if he could refill his water bottle. "Never mind, he's coming in."

Drake made our entire entryway look small, and his workout shirt said GET IT GET IT GET IT. I wasn't sure what IT was.

Dad nodded and stood there awkwardly. He'd offered to drive me to the gym, and I'd replaced him, and even though it was a small thing, he looked kind of lost.

"See you later," I told him. I watched him fall back into his chair with a thud, pulling his laptop onto his TV tray.

Drake opened the fridge to fill his water, and I noticed that my dad had thrown out all the weird processed sandwich meat. There was a new pot of some questionable vegetable sludge with chunks of meat that didn't exactly look cooked, just sunburned.

Was he trying to cook? Drake didn't say anything, but he spent a couple of seconds staring at the contents of our sad fridge. I cleared my throat pointedly and inclined my head toward the door.

"Does he like . . . speak?" Drake asked as he was getting back into his truck. He seemed even bigger in the truck.

"Not if he can help it," I said.

"So it's quiet all the time?" He was being inconveniently perceptive today, which was usually Evey's job.

I nodded.

"Dude. I'd die. You are both emotionally constipated."

I laughed, but he was right. All conversation is forced. It's not necessarily painful, just uncomfortable.

He's the only parent I have left.

The only person I live with.

The only family I have in this country.

And I can't tell him anything.

Drake turned the radio on full blast, and my heart rate immediately spiked. I reached out and turned the volume down, and Drake was irritated for about half a second but let it go.

"When Brad married my mom, we talked about

everything. EVERYTHING. He said he could deal with a lot from me. Bad grades. Attitude. Whatever. He said, just don't lie to me. So I don't. And that means he gets a shitload more information than he needs, but at least we talk."

"My dad isn't the talking type," I explained, holding on to my seat as Drake made a sharp turn and hit the curb.

"Yeah. Well, neither are you. Talk about that. Also, what's with your fridge? Do Greek people not eat food?"

Our fridge has definitely been going through some stuff. An evolution I can't explain. Yia Yia died, and after all the frozen trays of food from people at church were consumed, there were the occasional vegetables that my dad would buy. All of them could be eaten raw because neither of us would do anything that resembled cooking. There was always milk, yogurt, and butter for toast. But now vegetables have been appearing with fierce regularity, and I don't exactly know what they're doing there. Like, does Dad want to eat them? Are they there because it makes the fridge look like people live here, and that makes us look, by default, less pathetic?

At any rate, it's weird.

The weirdness of a bunch of strange food just sitting there occupying space Yia Yia used to fill.

If she was going to haunt us for anything, it would have to be the food.

She'd be so horrified by the TV dinners my dad filled our freezer with. She'd look at the frozen food and ask *What is it?* as if it were a fossil or a rock or somebody's ultrasound. And then she'd look at us and open her eyes wide when we explained that it is, in fact, food.

No, agapi mou. Not food. I know food. This isn't it.

For the record, she's right. I think the consumption of so much processed food over the past year has permanently altered my DNA. Maybe that's why my progress in yoga and basic self-defense has been slow. I mean, in addition to my lack of coordination.

Luckily, Drake has been reasonably patient. When we reached the gym, he made a point to outline everything we were going to do, and then, miraculously, he said very little as he adjusted my stance.

"Right hook."

"Uppercut."

"Roundhouse kick."

"Cover your face, Leo."

"Fix your stance, Leo."

"Excellent, now do that again, but better."

Through yoga and Drake's attempts to teach me a little self-defense, I've learned that I have (1) terrible posture and (2) very little chance of surviving a zombie apocalypse that Drake is 100 percent certain is going to happen and is really excited about.

"C'mon, dude, what would you do?" he asked, holding up a giant red foam board for me to punch. I spit out the blue mouth guard he made me buy and put it in its case before draining the last of my water.

"Die, I guess."

"No, like, seriously."

"You have a plan for a zombie apocalypse?" I asked, rubbing my face.

"It's only a matter of time, dude."

"Okay, what's your plan?"

He grins, rounds his shoulders slightly, and then says very seriously, "Costco."

"What?"

"I am setting up camp at Costco. Which means that whenever we get word of the illness taking over the planet or weird disappearances—I'm grabbing Jen and our parents and we're starting a new life at Costco. It's a warehouse store! Tons of food, outdoor furniture, barbecues—we'll be fine."

"Okay, then, why am I learning to fight zombies if we're just going to Costco?"

Drake laughed. "No, no, *I* am going to Costco. I don't know where you're going."

"I can't come?"

"I guess you can make blankets. . . ." He trailed off before clapping his hands, insisting that I put the mouth guard back in, and making me go again. When I finally sat on the mat with my now-empty water bottle, my body hurt.

I wasn't great, but I was actually getting a little better.

A few minutes later, Jen burst through the door and came running over to kiss Drake. Drake was sweaty, but that didn't seem to bother Jen as she threw her arms around him. I was trying not to throw up in my mouth. Evey had followed her in and was observing the physical contact with a look of disgust too as she sat down on the mat. Her hair was tied up in a ponytail, and she was wearing gray yoga pants and a black tank top.

"What's going on?" Jen asked.

"Leo wants to come to Costco," Drake said.

She glanced at me. "Is he . . . making blankets?"

"That's what I said!"

Then they kinda fell into a gross couple-y discussion about the end of the world, and that's when Evey interrupted by asking what we were practicing.

Drake rattled off the stuff he'd been showing me, then—

"Let's show them."

My stomach dropped.

"You're fine," he said. "You're doing way better. Besides, everyone sucks in the beginning."

So we ran through the motions and the punches. Drake corrected my footwork, and when we were done, Jen applauded, which felt a tiny bit patronizing. Luckily, I was in the mood to appreciate the support.

"Not bad," Evey finally said.

Her eyes were unreadable.

"Ready?" she asked me. I leaned over to pack up my stuff.

"Off on your secret adventure?" Jen asked.

"Yep," Evey said.

"Hey, what about quinoa?" Drake asked.

"Rain check!" said Evey. "I got Leo a sandwich."

I smiled triumphantly at Drake, who was clearly devastated.

"Don't worry, babe. I'll eat gross healthy food with you," said Jen.

"You said you liked quinoa," he said.

Evey nodded toward the door.

"Still won't tell us what it is?" Drake called out, twining his fingers around Jen's and kissing her hand.

"Let's go," said Evey, rolling her eyes at their semigross, semiadorable display of affection.

We got into Evey's car, and I thought I was prepared for awkward, but then I saw that she'd put the crocheted poo on the dashboard. I looked at it and grinned.

"This is weird, right?" I asked her.

"What's weird?" she said, putting on her seat belt.

"This arrangement. Where I help you create pictures for revenge, and in exchange you don't tell my dad I lied to him about the fight class."

"When you put it like that, I don't sound very nice," she said.

"Hence the poo."

"But," she said, pulling onto the freeway, "one could argue that this is the curse's doing. Not mine."

"One could. But they'd be wrong," I said. "Also, I'd give back the icon my great-great-grandfather stole if I could."

"But you can't," said Evey, smiling. "So maybe just help me do this."

She pulled off the freeway onto a road that led toward the water.

"Jordan has a boat?" I asked when we pulled up to a dock. Of course he had a boat. I'm sure I'd heard that somewhere. So far the only thing I knew for certain about this guy was that (1) he had a lot of expensive stuff and (2) he'd really pissed Evey off.

Evey grabbed a bag and was about to open the door when I leaned over her and held the door shut.

"Okay, wait. This doesn't involve stealing someone's boat, right? Because, like I said before, I'm not going to jail for this."

"It's not a boat," she said. "It's a Jet Ski. The boat is his dad's."

Which turned out to be huge.

"That doesn't answer my quest—"

"No, we're not stealing anything," Evey snapped.

"What did this guy do?" I asked. She didn't answer.

"He might be a douchebag. And he might even be conniving and creepy, but I think I should say again that this is pretty elaborate for a guy who just broke up with you."

Her eyes flashed dangerously. "You really don't know, do you?" she asked.

I shook my head. "And you're not going to tell me?"

She ignored me and got out of the car.

We walked along the dock, and I noticed names on the boats. WELLINGTON. REGINALD. They sounded expensive. Then we finally approached one monster that looked like it ate another boat. It said SWANSEA on the back, and it had its own private gate.

"Okay, how are you getting in?" I asked. It made no sense that she would have access to this boat.

147

She pulled a key out of her pocket.

"How did you get that?" I asked.

"If you pay attention," said Evey, "you can figure out just about anything."

Then she looked at me and sighed. "I know where they keep the spare key," she said. "We were together for months. You learn stuff."

"How do you get away with just saying shit like that?" I asked. "You just learn stuff? Like you just casually observe everyone at all times and collect information to use later?"

"Yes," she said. "And stop shouting. We're trying not to draw attention."

The dock was empty except for a few people walking their dogs and some joggers who didn't mind that it was overcast and chilly by the water, but Evey didn't seem to mind the people or the cold. We walked up the ramp to the boat like she was supposed to be there.

I pulled out the yarn, the camera, all the knitting projects I'd been working on, and a few white sheets that I thought we might use for a backdrop because I'd had no idea where we were going.

"How do you know they aren't going to show up?" I asked.

She lifted her head from the clothes she was pulling out of her backpack and pointed at the paint cans and mainte-nance tools on deck.

"They're repainting and installing new furniture below-decks. His family won't be here again for another few weeks."

"And you know this because . . . ?"

She pointed to the sign taped to a door to our left.

MAINTENANCE PERMIT.
ABSOLUTELY NO ADMITTANCE BEYOND THIS POINT.
WORK SCHEDULED THROUGH MARCH 31.

And I was feeling pretty confident that Evey knew what she was talking about and that we would take the pictures and just be on our weird, merry way until I heard someone talking on a walkie-talkie.

"Yeah. I'll check it out," said a voice before it cut out.

For the first time, Evey was clearly nervous.

"Shit," she whispered. "Move!" She pointed to a sliding door to our immediate right. It was the room with the steering wheel. Whatever that's called.

Confidence is a special kind of magic, because she'd made me completely forget that she'd had no idea we were in danger of being devoured by Jordan's giant beast dog and that I'd stupidly gone along for that ride as well without considering that MAYBE SHE DIDN'T KNOW EVERY-THING ALL THE TIME.

"In here," Evey whispered, grabbing all the stuff we'd unpacked and stuffing it inside before shutting us in the dark. The space wasn't really big enough for two people, but we managed to wedge in there with our bags and squeeze just beneath the window so no one would see us inside. Evey grabbed two life jackets from a pile in the corner and covered

149

us with them while footsteps crunched outside. The guard was a young white guy, maybe twenty-something, with a security vest and a flashlight on his belt. He peeked into the window of the door we were leaning against but thankfully did not try the door.

Breaking and entering. *Jesus Christ, we are going to jail. I can't go to jail,* I thought. *I can't pee in front of other people.*

My heart started to pound and I felt my hands getting sweaty. I wanted off this boat.

"It's just a security guard doing his rounds," Evey whispered. "He'll leave in a minute. I know him. Just relax."

"Like you knew Strudel?" I whisper-shouted at her, remembering the dog. I said, with my face in my hands, "If you know him, then we should just get out and make our presence known."

I'm not claustrophobic per se, but I don't enjoy the feeling of being trapped, so Evey talking us out of this was more appealing to me than hiding in a confined space.

She looked uncomfortable.

"He knows you shouldn't be here, right?"

She glared at me.

And I did that thing where I forget where I am and I muttered in Greek under my breath, forgetting that it isn't a secret code, since the other person trapped with me also speaks it.

"What was Yia Yia right about?"

"It doesn't matter," I said.

"You don't want to tell me?" she asked.

I rolled my eyes, hard. "No. Actually I don't. You're not exactly an open book about *anything,* so I don't really feel like sharing. Thanks."

Silence. Then—

"What do you want to know?" she whispered.

"Like you'll just tell me anything I want to know?" I asked her.

"Maybe," she said. "No harm in asking."

I scoffed.

"Okay. Sit there and say nothing," she said.

That sounded awful too.

"What's the deal with the magazines?" I asked in a whisper, remembering the stacks in the back of her car. "I've seen you with hundreds. And why are they all marked with Post-it notes?"

"Oh, that. I'm just trying to get published. I want to work for a big magazine someday, maybe as a travel journalist. So I send practice articles and pitches out all the time. The Post-it notes are for articles I like."

"So you write," I said.

"Well, yeah, but mostly I get rejections right now." And for a minute she actually lowered her gaze and looked shy about it.

It was profoundly weird hearing Evey talk about getting rejected, and she actually seemed vulnerable for a second.

"That's pretty cool," I said.

She smiled. A real smile.

So I blurted out, "Evey, why are we doing this?"

We were both still in the semidarkness. In this tiny room, neither of us really had to pretend.

"Why are we making this revenge artistic, and why does this matter? There are other ways to mess with somebody after you break up. You could spread rumors if you wanted, or you could find some other way to ruin him. Why use me? Why make it art? I don't get it."

Again she didn't answer, and I couldn't understand why she wouldn't just come out and tell me what happened.

"Look. He's probably garbage," I said. "Anyone with eyes can see that. Just by the way he acts around other people. Whatever he did, you didn't deserve it."

"Even if I blackmail someone into taking photos for a bizarre revenge plot?" she asked.

"Oh, good. You think it's bizarre too."

She laughed, and it was a welcome sound until I remembered we were supposed to be quiet.

"And the rest of the plan for these photos is what, exactly? I mean, I assume they're meant to be posted somewhere."

"Instagram," she said. "I have a separate account with thousands of followers from when I was trying to become an influencer. I have hashtags ready to go. And for the photo contest on your flyer, part of the process is to tag the contest's organization and the schools looking for photography students."

"Wait, what?" I said.

"You didn't know that was part of it? Getting schools to look at your work."

I shook my head stupidly.

"So what was Yia Yia right about?" she asked.

"Secrets and lies lead to bad luck. Also . . . to stay away from you."

Evey snorted and I shushed her, afraid the guard was still nearby.

"Stay away from me?"

"Well, stay away from your whole family," I said.

"You believe in curses?" she asked.

"I believe in bad luck," I said. "All your great-great-grandmother said was 'I hope you burn in hell.' And then Stavros died in a fiery car crash."

Evey thought about this and nodded. "Yeah. Sometimes stuff just works out."

"So you're not going to tell me what Jordan did? The real thing he did?" I asked.

"The guard is gone," she said. "Let's get out there."

She opened the door, and I followed her back onto the deck quietly as she crept down the ladder at the back of the boat and uncovered a Jet Ski with the word JUNIOR emblazoned on the side. I grimaced.

"Yeah, he hated that too. His dad put that on there."

"Whatever floats his boat." I waggled my eyebrows at her. A smile tugged at her lips, though she tried to hide it. "So, do you have a vision for this one?"

When she didn't say anything, I pulled the letters out of my bag. Two *Es*, a *T,* an *A,* an *H,* an *R,* and a *C*. Weird that she didn't tell me what the word was going to be this time, but maybe that was part of the process. I was supposed to create something in the moment.

I pulled my yarn out of my bag, and Evey pulled the stuff out of hers. A stack of books and a lacy black tank top. Huh. I looked at the letters again.

H–E–T–C–E–A–R

Then rearranged them.

C–H–E–A–T–E–R

Actually, this one was pretty simple.

When I got behind the camera, the story was more painful for Evey. She held the lacy tank top at the end of her fingertip, and even though I could tell she was trying to be brave and trying to show Jordan's character, there was a lot of hurt there too.

The pictures I took captured the way she moved between anger and sadness. There were a few moments where she even looked embarrassed by what she was holding and where she was sitting. Maybe even what we were doing there.

And it was a new experience for me as a photographer.

My go-to place for taking pictures is a cemetery.

And to be honest, most of my photos aren't of human subjects. I like nature and animals and weird broken stuff that tells a story. But I don't usually take photos of people.

Watching Evey through my camera lens made me realize that people change by the second. Every expression means something, and every moment captured can tell a different story.

We'd missed the golden hour. The best light for photography. The gorgeous moment just before the light vanishes, where pictures make the subjects look larger than life. Mythical, even. But the photos still turned out surprisingly good.

"Got it?" she asked.

"Got it," I said.

"Great, let's get out of here."

I hadn't put my camera down yet. I'm glad I hadn't, because after we put everything away, I caught a smile like the one she'd had when she talked about wanting to write for magazines.

Evey Paros genuinely happy.

I captured the moment, and it was impossible not to look at that and smile too.

Namaste,
Leo

15

Today's Pose: Dancer

Stand up.

Lift your foot into the palm of your hand behind you and raise your other arm.

Hinge forward still holding your foot and trust your body to bend into a perfect bow.

This is one of the poses that look easy but aren't.

That moment when you can hinge all the way forward holding your body into a perfect bow—that's pretty graceful. And I'm not there yet, but I can hold my foot up and start the bend.

Progress.

Drake would be so proud.

Dear Journal,

I woke up to a text from Drake.

> Are you hiding cereal?

> Lucky Charms?!

> Fat Leo rides again . . .

> Sorry about that nickname by the way. I was going through some stuff and it wasn't cool. I won't ever use that again.

Shit. Drake was in my kitchen.

> Why are you in my kitchen?

> Your dad said I could wait for you.

That didn't answer my question, but suddenly "Eye of the Tiger" was blaring outside my bedroom door.

"Dude. I am not running with you. Ever."

"You don't have to. But you need to get your ass up so we can train. Early yoga today, remember?"

I hadn't remembered. But I got dressed, mumbled

something to my dad about where we were going, and followed Drake out the door.

I discovered when we got to the gym that Drake had asked Evey to help with a roundhouse kick demonstration because hers is the best he's ever seen. And he was right. It was impressive.

We watched her beat the piss out of a rubber dummy. Her leg went up and into his face like the side of a battering ram, again and again in rapid succession. And she hit the same part of the dummy's head every time.

Drake and I didn't speak. He silently lifted his phone out of his pocket to record the last twenty seconds but almost dropped it when she stopped and turned around to face us. She had this crazed, manic look on her face, and Drake just said, "Thank you, Evey," as she walked out into the hall to fill her water bottle.

When I moved forward to get ready to try it myself, Drake put his hand on the dummy and with a serious face said, "Give him a minute, dude. He just went through some stuff."

Then he looked at me thoughtfully for a second.

"I wish I could punch you," he said.

"What? Why?" I asked, looking at him.

"I mean, part of defending yourself is learning what your body can handle. So if you got punched, you wouldn't be so tense about it."

"Dude. We've been over this. You did punch me. I fell down. They sent us to the equivalent of high school couples therapy."

"Right," he said. "Well, next time don't fall down."

I actually don't fall down much anymore.

I've lost weight and I've become, I dunno . . . swifter? I'm not a ninja or anything, but I feel like I move more gracefully, with purpose. I don't drop stuff as much, and I actually do feel faster. But unfortunately this has zero effect on my dancing ability, as I discovered at pageant practice later that day.

Traditional Greek dance is not really difficult. It's not really the most beautiful dance in the world either. But it is pretty happy if done right. It's also considerably more successful when you don't watch your feet or worry about crushing people.

You raise your arms and move back and forth in a line with the group, and it's just as much about the energy of the people you're dancing with as it is about the steps.

Forward. Backward. Arms raised. Feet moving at exactly the same time.

I'd been given a pass on the dance portion of the pageant from my Yia Yia for years. The thought of messing up and ruining the group Kalamata dance was terrifying—not because I cared at all about footwork or authenticity; I just didn't want everyone looking at me when I screwed it all up. That's a panic-inducing moment that I would not be able to undo. But my Yia Yia had not written my note this year. Being dead made that difficult. And when I tried to broach the subject with Dad, he just said, "If everyone else has to dance, so do you."

Thanks.

And that was it. No discussion.

So I waited, trying not to get worked up. Trying not to hold my stomach in, which was impossible.

Then rehearsal started and the music started up and we all squashed together like a herd of goats and moved awkwardly to the beat.

Predictably, everyone else got it after a couple of seconds. Somehow their Greekness pulled them through it, like the blood of their ancestors propelled them forward to dance the dance of freedom.

I, on the other hand, began to sway awkwardly, which was disappointing because I thought maybe some of the grace acquired through yoga might have helped, but no.

That's when I felt Evey's hand take mine.

She called out to our teacher and told her I was supposed to be taking pictures for the website. When Mrs. Anagamas was unconvinced, Evey fixed her with a very persuasive look that said she was both irritated with her and completely in control of the situation.

I wanted to laugh at how easy it was for her to get people to do what she wanted. Minus blackmail, of course.

"Go," Evey said.

I disappeared behind the lens of my camera and immediately felt lighter. There's so much freedom in being able to capture a moment, like I can be a part of it without feeling anxious.

And after a lot of awkward movement, everyone disbanded. I packed up my bag and got my camera ready to go too.

Evey was still there, and she watched me pack up my stuff. I turned away, but when I looked back, she was still watching me.

"May I help you?" I asked in what I thought was a pretty decent attempt at being cool and carefree.

She lifted her hands toward me.

"What?" I asked.

"Let me show you," she said.

"Show me what?"

She took my hand.

She started to guide me through the steps. Back and forth, in the circle that everyone else had figured out on their own. I didn't look down at my feet. I stared at our hands and then I looked at Evey, who wasn't smiling, but she did look happy. She wasn't the kind of person who *did* happy like everyone else anyway. She looked busy and determined. *That* was genuinely happy for her. Then we stopped dancing and she twirled away from me triumphantly.

I was waiting for her to say something like "You worry too much" or "See, you *can* do it!" or "Look what happens when you finally relax." But she didn't. The circumstance was different, and it still wasn't a natural, effortless thing for me to dance. But I did not fall down.

"You look happy," I mused. "Did you get a response from one of the magazines?"

"Yep. Rejections from *Teen Beat, Teen Vogue, Fitness*

magazines. Also these," she said. Then she reached into her bag and handed me a stack of others she was saving.

"That usually doesn't make people happy, though," I said.

Dear Ms. Paros,

While I enjoyed your pieces, I feel that your work ultimately lacked the personal connection we crave in our writers, and to be perfectly honest, you don't have the experience necessary to qualify for our internship program just yet.

Thank you for your interest!
Best of luck!

Dear Ms. Paros,

Your writing is underdeveloped, and no one wants to read a sad story about a little Greek flower girl. I don't care enough about this story.

Thanks for your interest!

Dear Writer,

Thank you for your interest. This is a courtesy email letting you know that we have received your email and will be reviewing your submission.

Dear Ms. Paros,

We regret to inform you . . .

"Oh," I said. "Sorry."

"It's okay," she said. "It's a response, at least! At least I have something to work on. A personal connection and higher stakes in my work. Let's try this again," she said, taking my hands and guiding me through the steps.

Not everyone is easy to figure out. It feels like Evey is just starting to let me in, but maybe not in the same way anyone else would. Like Drake or Jen.

Note: I wish Jen and Drake grossed me out more. But they're actually kinda adorable. Most high school couples are unnatural, but Jen and Drake completely embrace their weirdness. Jen is unashamedly in love with calculus, and Drake is on a quest to rid the world of processed food. Somehow it works.

When Evey finished a final twirl, she caught my eye, and before she let go of my hand, she squeezed it.

"I think you're doing better," she said.

I think so too.

Namaste,
Leo

16

No pose today. Annabelle is sick. No class.

Dear Journal,

I'm writing this because I was supposed to train with Drake and then go to yoga as usual. But then Drake was late, so I pulled out the sweatbands I was making for the girls' cross-country team. I'd just started to work when I got his text.

Sorry, dude. I ate ice cream.

And . . . ?

Jesus, Leo. I can't just eat ice cream.

I'm super lactose intolerant.

Okay, then why . . . ?

The heart wants what
the heart wants, bro.

I didn't know how to respond to this, but luckily I didn't
have to.

Jen and her mathlete friends
went to a new gelato place
and there was a strawberry
cheesecake ice cream with
like real pieces of crust in
it and it was a cheat day
and I thought I had my gas
pills in my bag with me
but I didn't. So long story
short. I ate ice cream and
my butt is a volcano of shit
lava and wicked gas. So I
gotta cancel training today.

I don't even know how I would begin to tell him that's
not necessarily something you need to share with someone else. Ever. So I texted back telling him not to worry
about it, and then I realized Evey was watching me from
the door.

"You do that everywhere?" she asked, looking at the yarn.

I nodded as she sat down next to me on the floor.

"It helps you relax," she said.

I shrugged.

"Because I noticed your arms don't tense up as much when you do it. You kinda transform into goo. Your face changes too."

Drake texted me a selfie of himself sitting on the toilet giving a thumbs-up, with a smiley face strategically placed over his crotch, and I tried to click it off my phone before Evey saw it. I wasn't quick enough, though.

"I used to think that was weird," Evey said, considering the photo. "But he just likes letting everyone know what he's thinking the minute he's thinking it. And he's not embarrassed by anything. Not a terrible trait, I guess."

She was leaning toward me, and ordinarily I would have been able to go back to my knitting, but she was looking at me expectantly.

"So no training with Drake and no yoga," she said.

"Yeah," I said, rolling up my yarn. There was no point in trying to knit now.

"You going to go knit somewhere?" she asked.

I grinned.

"I was thinking of grabbing my camera and taking some pictures, actually."

"Can I come?" she asked.

I accidentally dropped one of my needles. "You want to come with me?" I asked, raising an eyebrow.

"Yeah, if that's okay," she said. "Do you have a favorite spot?"

"Yeah," I said, trying to think of some place way cooler than the cemetery. "It's just not . . . I dunno."

I couldn't figure out how to finish the sentence. *Not normal,* maybe?

"Well, I'm free for a bit if you don't mind company. Unless the place is, like, dangerous or something." She looked like she didn't believe I would actually go anywhere dangerous, but she was giving me the benefit of the doubt.

"No, it's just a place I like to go. It's kinda . . . I dunno. Creepy and beautiful."

I realized after I said it how stupid that sounded, but Evey didn't laugh or scoff or look away. She was genuinely curious.

"Where?" she asked.

"It's hard to explain," I said.

"Can you show me?" she asked. I felt my stomach tense up again, and I leaned back.

"Not if it's a secret, though," she added.

"No, it's not—" I said quickly.

"Well, if you're going anyway, take me on a field trip."

"Why?" I asked.

She smiled. "Feels like a secret. I like secrets."

• • •

"So you hang out with dead people," Evey said when we got to the cemetery.

"I mean, they're here. I'm not exactly sure we hang out," I said.

I'm not really sure at what moment Evey realized where I was taking her. Maybe when I told her to follow the line of hearses making their way in a funeral procession to the oldest mausoleum at the back of the grounds.

She parked her car at the bottom of a winding path and turned off the engine.

"I'm just tagging along. So just do whatever it is that you do."

It was weirdly personal all of a sudden. I couldn't quite figure out why she wanted to come.

"It usually just starts with a walk. People leave all kinds of weird things at cemeteries. So I just walk until I find something."

"Let's go," she said.

Evey trailed along behind me, looking around, glancing at the occasional tombstone. I found an umbrella someone had propped against a headstone. A book left on a bench. A scarf. And a tiny shovel someone had left stabbed into the ground.

For a minute I forgot Evey was there until she came up behind me and asked, "Don't you ever take pictures of people?"

"I can't do that here," I said.

It was partially a respect thing and partially an I-don't-want-to-talk-to-people-if-I-don't-have-to thing.

"I mean, obviously you don't walk up to the people who are sobbing, but what about the people sitting by themselves or the people who work here. They might—"

I shook my head.

"What if I ask?'

I tilted my head and considered her.

"Sure. You get someone to agree and I'll do it."

We rounded a corner and there was a man sitting with his little fluffy white dog under a jacaranda tree bursting with purple flowers. Evey watched him for half a second, seemed to determine that it was safe to approach, and sat down next to him.

She introduced herself, and even though I couldn't hear everything they were saying, I could tell she was getting his life story. She pulled out a notebook, wrote a few things down, and waved me over.

"This is Leo," she said. "Leo, this is Carl. He's visiting his wife. He says it's okay if you take his picture."

It could not be clearer that she was smug about this. She stood up and said to Carl, "Just do exactly what you were doing before."

"Just talking to my wife," he said.

I nodded.

He turned back to the tombstone and began talking, but I wasn't listening to the conversation. I watched as his dog perked up a little and edged closer to where Carl had laid down a bouquet of flowers.

Every movement told a story. The way he touched his wedding band. The way the dog reacted every time Carl said his wife's name.

I snapped a few more photos of the two of them and thanked him for his time before we walked on.

"Try her," said Evey.

It was a woman with a clipboard. Then a gardener. Then a hearse driver. They all said yes.

I glanced down at my camera and then back at Evey.

"Then I usually knit for a while," I said.

"Any particular spot?"

We walked to Yia Yia's grave, near a garden path by the lake.

"How often do you come here?" Evey asked me.

"When I need to," I said. It wasn't an answer, but it felt like the only one worth giving.

"And you just take photos here?"

"Mostly."

"What do you do the rest of the time?"

"Try to remember."

"Remember what?"

"What it felt like to not worry. About anything."

She took my hand.

"This was really cool," she said.

"But also creepy, right?" I asked.

"Not as creepy as I thought it would be. It's quiet. Pretty peaceful. I can see why you come here," she said.

"But . . . ?"

She smiled. "But you can find quiet around people too."

She drove me home, and before I could overthink it, I kissed her on the cheek and got out.

Namaste,
Leo

17

Today's Pose: Supported Headstand

Our instructor tells us it's supposed to strengthen the whole body and calm the mind. Probably because all the blood comes rushing to your head and you hear it pulsing around your ears.

But maybe there's some spiritual shit to it too.

Everyone else in the room does it immediately on their mats, and I sort of just stare at them like they're a weird family of bats going down for the night.

But Annabelle smiles and escorts me to the back of the room. She shows me how to make a cradle for my head with my hands and forearms, and then tells me to kick up against a wall.

As usual, I think she's going to have to physically lift

my legs up against the wall. But I clench my stomach in and manage to do it myself this time. Without falling over.

And for a few minutes we are weird bats together.

Dear Journal,

My dad put his hand on my shoulder yesterday when I got home from the cemetery.

This isn't a big deal in the grand scheme of things, but talking with my dad is a little bit like talking with a favorite rock, so the fact that he expressed any kind of closeness or emotion at all is amazing.

And it made me happy for, like, a split second before my mind started racing with stuff. It wasn't even bad stuff. It was just stuff clinging to the pipeline into my brain, making all other thought impossible until I was breathing hard. Like I'd been running, but I was standing perfectly still, and my chest hurt.

But the thoughts kept swirling and bobbing in and out of my head. It's like when you wake up from a dream and then suddenly you can't remember what it was about and you waste all this time thinking about it only to discover that the thing you fixated on remembering was a squirrel or something equally stupid.

Then I got a text from Evey.

Hey

Yes?

You're off the hook. I'm not going to make you take any more pictures or do any more yarn-bombing.

Okay.

But if you want to, I have one more idea. Something that would round out your submission for the contest, I think. But it's definitely riskier. There's a bigger chance we'll get caught. And when he finds out, he'll be pissed.

But I could use your help.

Okay. I'm in.

That's it?

That's it.

Why?

Because you weren't a jerk about it this time.

Namaste,
Leo

173

18

Today's Pose: Tree

Standing upright on one leg while pulling the bottom of your other foot into your thigh.

This is one of those moments when I'm reminded of my class-pet status because this is the kind of pose that people have been nailing for years and yet Annabelle still feels the need to say, "Be sure not to rest your foot on the inside of your knee."

Because that's exactly where my foot is. And I know she's not saying that for anyone else.

Dear Journal,

I saw Jordan at lunch when I went to sit with Drake, which wouldn't have been unusual except that he seemed to see me too. He broke off from his friends to run over to me. Not real running. The fake kind that looks like you're in a hurry to catch someone.

"Got another order for you," he said.

He smiled and handed me his phone, which had a pattern for a woman's shawl. The stitchwork was intricate, and the model in the magazine was wearing it low, revealing a lot of skin.

"I'll pay whatever you want, but I need it in a week. I'll text the image to you." Then he winked. He was about to walk off like it was a done deal, but I stopped him.

"Sorry, man," I said. "I have a ton of orders to finish. Should open up in a week, though."

His smile faltered and turned into a smirk. "You sure? Price isn't an issue."

"I'm sure," I said. Then something clicked into place. His smile vanished, and he retreated toward his pack.

Evey's eyes met mine from the opposite side of the quad as she disappeared past a row of lockers.

"Can someone tell me what actually happened between them?" I asked Drake. "Everyone knows but me."

Jen sighed but didn't say anything.

"He played her," Drake said.

"Played Evey?"

It didn't seem possible that someone like Evey could be played.

"I know, right?" said Jen, reading my mind. "She liked being popular. She wasn't in love with him or anything, but she liked him at first, and everything that came with dating him. Like the attention. And she didn't listen when I told her he was a douchebag."

"When *everyone* told her he was a douchebag," Drake corrected.

"So what did he do?" I asked.

"I can't believe you don't know," Jen said, genuinely surprised. I shook my head, realizing that it must have been common knowledge at school.

"No," said Drake. "Leo doesn't enjoy people. He doesn't know."

"He made it a game," Jen said. "He dated Evey, then he made it a game to see how many other girls he could get with without her knowing. It just . . . hit her a little late."

There was something on Jen's face that was tricky to read. But if I had to make a guess, I'd say she was still a little bit mad at Evey. Like she wanted to be supportive, but the effort of not saying *I told you so* was taking almost all her concentration.

"Why didn't *you* tell her?" I asked Drake. It seemed completely out of character for him to not share information. I mean, he does it with strangers.

"I knew he was an asshole, but I honestly didn't know about the other girls. I found out about that right when she did."

"The water polo guys kept it a secret," Jen interjected. "Assholes. But like I said, she didn't want to hear it anyway. She was happy and popular. Nominated for Homecoming Court. So when it happened, it kinda smacked her in the face. And he joked about everything. Everything they did together. And I mean *everything*." Jen shook her head.

"So in conclusion," said Drake, "she has trust issues."

It made me think of something Yia Yia always said. She was full of Greek proverbs. *He who has been burned by hot milk blows on yogurt.*

"I think I'll go find her," I told Jen and Drake.

I had walked out of the quad and through the rows of lockers where I thought she'd gone, when I heard a voice.

"Look, I don't know what you're planning, but whatever it is, you can't touch me," said Jordan.

"Don't worry," Evey said. "I never want to touch you again."

He laughed. It was a very distinctive laugh, forced and loud, and instantly recognizable.

"Are you okay?" I said when Jordan's footsteps had disappeared.

"No," she said.

I held out my hand and she took it as we walked back to Drake and Jen.

When we got close, they went conspicuously quiet. Like idiots.

"Talking about me?" Evey asked, raising an eyebrow but not looking particularly concerned.

"Yep," said Jen.

Evey and Jen looked at each other, and Evey smiled. And I knew the smile conveyed way more than Drake and I could possibly understand. And I was immediately jealous.

I wish I could communicate like that. With a look, and then complete understanding.

I don't think anyone has ever looked at me with complete understanding.

Then I remembered something. "Here," I said, handing Evey a yellow tulip I'd made last night.

"I deserve flowers now?" she asked.

I smiled and said nothing.

Namaste,
Leo

19

Today's Pose: Camel

Start by kneeling. Then I'm told to rotate my thighs inward slightly, and I still have no idea what the hell that means.

Then narrow my hip points without hardening my buttocks.

It is at this point that my butt cheeks clench like they're trying to pick up a quarter, because they don't like being told what to do.

Then walk your hands slowly all the way down your back and lift your chest.

Try not to think about how this pose is actually torture.

Dear Journal,

I started teaching Drake to knit during our time in Mr. Thomas's room, and so far it's been like toilet training a cat.

He has zero focus, and he manages to tangle the yarn or drop the needles or do both every time, so we moved on to crocheting for now, which is working out pretty well if you know anyone who wants long, uneven chains of yarn that look like they were made by drunk toddlers. At least he's making something and he hasn't given up yet. That's progress. He continued crocheting one long rope. I was about to tell him that we needed to learn how to do the second row because what he was doing wasn't actually crocheting, but then he looked up and went:

"This is fun, Leo. Thanks for teaching me."

Mr. Thomas was obviously trying not to burst into tears. Tears of smugness, if that's possible.

I avoided meeting his eyes and focused instead on the letters Evey had asked me to make over a week ago.

I crocheted them in bright red fuzzy yarn. It was clear what they would spell, so I didn't have to ask her this time. *Asshole* is a pretty distinct word. And I had another bag full of other projects she'd asked me to bring. Half-finished projects. Squares.

Then she sent me a text while I was sitting with Drake.

Can you do it tonight?
Last one, I promise.

I'm in if you are.

"I hope you guys know what you're doing," said Drake, who was now wrapping his crocheted chains around his arms like a weird cocoon.

"Me too," I said.

• • •

Evey was not as composed as she'd been before our other photo shoots. It was strange being the calm one for a change. I didn't like the responsibility. It felt like an extra weight in my stomach, but I forced conversation because she was muttering to herself in Greek and I thought maybe she'd like to talk to someone else. Maybe she'd like to look a little bit more together.

"Why is this one different?" I asked. "You weren't nervous at all for the other ones."

"I'm not nervous," she said impatiently. "This one is just bigger. It's going to take more time." She ran her nails along the steering wheel. I knew it was better to just wait for her to get to the point. Interrupting her internal monologue was just going to piss her off.

"It's his car," she said finally.

"We're yarn-bombing a car?"

"After we get it towed," she said.

I thought I'd seen an absurdly expensive-looking car in the school parking lot. That had to be his.

"Wow," I said. "How are we accomplishing this?"

She leaned back when we got to a stoplight. "The

parking lot spaces in the covered garage are all labeled with the owner's name on a little plaque. The parking lot attendants just scan all the plates to make sure they match the name. If your license plate doesn't match, you get towed."

"So you switched the plaque?"

Evey smiled.

"So when Jordan goes looking for his Mercedes—"

"Maserati," Evey said.

"Right . . . it won't be there? We just wait for it to get towed to an impound lot?"

"It's already been towed," she said.

I whistled.

"The impound lot owner is a woman. I explained the situation, and she's letting us in."

"That's it?" I asked.

"She said we gotta stick together."

"And she's just letting you yarn-bomb an impounded Maserati so that when he picks it up—"

"His parents. When his parents pick it up. They're the ones who own it, so they have to go get it."

"Oh," I said, because I couldn't think of what else to say.

"You want out?" she asked.

"No," I said quickly. But I'm not sure why. It was perfectly reasonable to want out.

"You're not under any obligation to help with this. I can set a timer on my phone and—"

I pretended to clutch my chest and made a very exaggerated, offended look. "A timer photo? That's what you'd replace me with? How could you?"

She grinned.

At the impound lot, the owner, a white woman with yellow hair and glitter eye shadow, opened the gates for us. It was grimy, and there was a definite feeling of abandonment there. Like all the cars were sad, but she was pretty high-energy, smiling the whole time we worked. Her name was Rena.

"I'm just going to tell them that this is how the car arrived," she said with a laugh. And she winked at Evey.

Then she laughed again when I pulled out all the yarn and the half-finished projects we were going to use to cover the car.

We started with the rows of pink granny squares I'd made for a blanket order that got canceled. Then we moved on to the skinny Christmas scarves I'd made years ago for church. Then the hats and discarded socks, and then finally the thick yarn ropes I'd made from all the sparkly yarn I had from some Halloween decorations I'd helped Yia Yia make for a church thing.

This great sense of calm washed over me. It was art. I had the design in mind, and I had everything I needed to work. Suddenly the rhythm clicked into place and I was wrapping yarn across the car like a spider, with Evey reaching out occasionally to take it from me and hand it back. Every now and then our fingers would touch, and Evey didn't seem to notice.

I did, though.

Rena had pulled an ancient chair outside to watch us work, and every so often she laughed, especially when the giant pink bra was strapped across the windshield over the yarn ropes we'd wrapped around the mirrors.

"I got an ex too, honey. He deserved worse than a yarn car, but this woulda been fun," she said.

After about two hours the car was covered. Not an inch of space could be seen through the yarn.

I arranged the letters, and Evey sat on the hood and looked directly at the camera, half a smile on her face. I knew immediately—that was the shot I'd use for my portfolio. Triumphant. Fierce. But we did spend a few minutes staging other shots of her appearing to attack the car with various crap around the lot.

Then she reached out her hand from the roof that she was now sitting on and said, "Take one with me."

I lowered my camera.

"Please?" she said.

Rena raced over to take the camera, and I climbed awkwardly up the yarn-covered car and sat down.

Evey leaned against my shoulder, and Rena took the pictures.

"You better get out of here before you get caught," she said, and we scrambled off the car, thanked her, and ran for it.

"So we're leaving it covered?" I asked, looking at all the yarn covering the car.

"Yeah," Evey said. "No turning back now."

I nodded, pulling a memory card out of the camera. "The photos," I said, handing it over. "These are the best ones. Pick your favorites."

She took it from me and smiled. "Thanks, Leo."

Except she said it in Greek.

And she didn't say Leo.

She said Leonidas.

Namaste,
Leo

20

Today's Pose: Locust

Also called one of the baby backbends. I'm told this is a simple pose that is actually very complex, which is actually my favorite kind because I don't have to worry about opening up my heart or my body or my mind or even my eyes if I don't feel like it. It's easy. You just hold still on the ground, on your belly, and keep your hands down by your sides.

Then the pose is ruined when Annabelle tells us, "Firm your buttocks so your coccyx presses toward your pubis."

And I realize I never want to hear the word pubis *again.*

Lift your head, upper torso, arms, and legs away from the floor. Rest on your lower ribs and belly and front pelvis. Firm your buttocks.

Do not jut chin forward.
Keep neck long.
Hold pose for thirty seconds to eternity.

Dear Journal,

There are days when the universe really does come through. And today it started with yoga.

I think I'd liken it to learning how to walk. Not that I remember that.

But ever since starting yoga, I haven't been able to get through an entire class without someone needing to fix my stance.

Today it was almost like I could feel them doing it before it happened.

I got into tree pose, and usually Annabelle would come racing over on tiptoe to help me raise my foot into my thigh, but all I could hear this time was a few quiet footsteps, then nothing as she watched me do it myself.

Then the same thing happened a few minutes later with crow pose.

Then a handstand.

I heard Annabelle's voice, just like I heard it every time.

"Kick and float your body up."

Usually this was followed by my body falling to the ground with a thud. But not today.

I kicked, then floated into the air, and for a second my body was straight as a board and all my muscles felt like they were moving into place as I rose. Then they melted together as I rolled my body down to the floor.

When I stood up, Annabelle was smiling. Everyone else was smiling too. I guess they'd noticed the lack of a falling body.

And I couldn't help it.

I smiled too.

And the universe wasn't even done yet. Even the March 25 pageant was better than usual.

I'd never really enjoyed March 25.

Until this weekend.

It was one of Yia Yia's favorite days in our house. Easter was big, but that was more about red eggs and Jesus. March 25 was about Greece.

She missed Greece more than anything, I think, and it was always hard for her to come back whenever we went home. We all called it home, even though I'd never lived there.

Anyway, she missed it, but she never talked about it much because I don't think she wanted me to think she regretted coming to live with us. But on Independence Day you could feel it. You could feel the sadness, the longing for connection. She was homesick, and she knew she'd never go back for good, not as long as she felt like we needed her here.

And if you looked at us, you knew we needed her.

This was the first March 25 without her, but it was the best one I've ever had. It feels cruel to say, because Yia Yia isn't here, but I think she'd understand, given the circumstances.

My dad and I showed up to church as usual. We sat next to each other. We didn't speak.

Evey was there with her parents, who were mingling with all the other Greek families.

"Leo," Evey called. She was wearing the full traditional clothing with the loose peasant top and deep wine-colored skirt with a white apron and head scarf over her hair. And there was something free about her.

I smiled.

"Dance with me," she said, and my smile faltered.

"We don't have to," I said quickly, pointing back at the camera I was going to use as my excuse.

"Dance with me," she said again. "Please?"

I think the really scary thing about dancing is not knowing the steps. Not knowing how to move forward and how to jump back in if you fall out of line, but she'd already danced with me. So I knew that even if I couldn't do it as part of a group, I could dance with her. Evey's confidence was contagious.

And for a moment, we were Greek. We twirled as our ancestors twirled. We ate as our ancestors ate. Too much lamb and potatoes. We spoke in raised voices, shouting like we were angry, even though we weren't.

Everything felt relaxed and even the usual surge of confusion that choked me at events like this was still. Still and listening, waiting to erupt into something later. But I didn't care because I felt connected to something.

Then Evey and I went outside. Nobody was there but us.

She didn't seem like the same person I'd known a few weeks ago. And I guess I wasn't the same person either.

"So I guess you won't be requiring my services anymore now that the photos are taken and you can post," I said, looking at her.

"No, you're right. Your services are no longer required." She looked up at the row of Greek flags draped all over the elaborate tent outside, where the microphones for the speeches had been set up hours before. "They're perfect, by the way. The photos, I mean. They're . . . exactly what I need."

There was something vulnerable about the way she said it, and then the wind picked up and all the flags waved in the breeze.

"I remember what you said before. At that party I dragged you to—"

"Don't worry about it," I said. "I don't care about that anymore."

"You said don't kiss me unless you mean it."

Her head scarf had come down.

I didn't say anything. I just watched her lean toward me and felt her lips on mine.

A real kiss this time.

Just us.

Kissing someone on March 25.

The universe really delivered this time.

Namaste,
Leo

190

21

No yoga. Annabelle on yoga retreat.

Dear Journal,

Getting woken up by Drake's texts is becoming a habit.

You kissed her?!?!

No.

That's not what my
intelligence tells me.

She kissed me.

Whatever, dude. That's huge.

> How did this happen?

> I have no idea.

> You can tell me tonight at the bonfire.

> Oh. Am I going to a bonfire?

> Evey says she's picking you up. It's just the basketball team, some of Jen's mathlete friends, a few people Evey knows from the gym, and like twenty of our closest friends.

I grimaced at the phone but smiled when Evey texted me a second later.

• • •

That evening our feet crunched against the sand as the breeze picked up on our way to the fire pits.

"Does anyone but me know about the yarn-bombing?" I asked her.

"They do now," she said.

"You posted?!"

"Picked three favorites and went for it," she said.

"I wonder how they'll react," I said, and she smiled.

"Two thousand likes since this morning," she said. "And I tagged you, even though your sad page only has, like, twenty pictures. You really should update that."

Two thousand likes, I thought.

When we got to the fire pits, Drake was throwing wood on the fire. Someone had made a jungle juice that tasted like Hawaiian Punch and vomit, but I held the cup so my hands would have something to do and so I wouldn't be tempted to stare at my phone when all the people got to be too much.

I'd left my camera at home, on purpose, but I regretted it almost immediately because the bonfire lighting was exceptional.

The yellows and oranges and reds, even the purples that erupted when Drake threw in a piece of a shipping pallet that was definitely not supposed to be burned. I took mental pictures, focused on what everyone was doing with their hands. Tried to focus on the feeling of being included and comfortable.

A camera wouldn't have been able to capture that.

"Stop taking pictures for a minute," Evey said. She was smiling and holding her own red cup and not drinking.

"It's that obvious?" I asked. We sat down on the benches set up around the fire.

There were a lot of people, but being outside helped. People were eating, drinking, leaning over each other to talk, and even though it was loud, it wasn't annoyingly loud. It was like our voices were crashing with the waves, and I felt okay with that.

Then Drake stood next to me with an uncharacteristi-cally serious look on his face.

"You really shouldn't have done that, Evey." Drake was always moving, and today was no exception. He was standing up, loading firewood, and as he was talking to us he was kinda bouncing on his feet. "Look. I told you. Jordan is a dick, but he's also the kind of dick who gets ugly when he's mad."

"I know that," Evey said. "I'm not afraid of him."

Drake was nervous, and it actually made him look small for the first time ever.

"You don't understand," he said.

"No, YOU don't understand," Evey said. "He's a creep. If posting some pictures that don't even prove anything freaks him out, then it's just because he's scared. Because he knows what he did."

Drake shook his head and was about to say something when Jen nudged him and said they needed more wood for the fire. He gave Evey another serious look before running off to his car to get more firewood.

It was late in the evening, but most of the girls were wearing bikinis under their clothes just in case. The guys were all in shorts. Then when the breeze picked up, almost everyone threw on a sweatshirt. Some of the basketball girls even pulled on the beanies I'd made.

Jen was sitting on a folding beach chair next to Drake's bag, and the basketball team had spread a sea of blankets on the sand, covering them with tiny coolers. One girl had brought an inflatable couch that had gotten too close to the fire and melted and now sat like a sad heap next to the coolers while takeout bags of burritos were being circulated around the group.

The mellow, hippie beach vibe was nice. And completely destroyed when Jordan and five other water polo guys showed up.

Then it went quiet.

Even the waves made slightly less noise.

"Did you think you were being funny with those photos?" Jordan said.

"Actually I—" Evey started to say.

"I wasn't talking to you," he said coldly. Then he turned the full force of his gaze on me. "Did you think it was funny?"

"I— It wasn't meant to be funny," I said.

"Did you think you might matter if you took them?"

I stood up, feeling the eyes of everyone in the group on me like a physical weight on my body. My brain froze and I suddenly forgot how to speak. The guys he brought with him were big, and they flanked him. All of them looking at me like I was dinner.

It wasn't the usual feeling I associated with anxiety. There was a funny taste in my mouth and a strange buzzing in my ears, which I stupidly thought meant I might be dealing with this.

I didn't even feel the first sucker punch.

I heard Evey scream at Jordan to stop, and I saw the rest of the team move in to block us from view or maybe from other people getting in the way. I don't know.

I tried to stand up, but I still couldn't breathe.

My face was suddenly in the sand, and I tasted blood in my mouth. Somewhere above me I could hear laughter. I could hear Jen and Evey both trying to get them to stop.

I pushed myself off the ground and brushed most of the sand off my face just in time to see Jordan lunge forward. For a second, I heard Annabelle telling me to root myself in the earth, and I heard Drake telling me to keep my thumb out of my fist. But neither of them seemed particularly helpful in the moment.

I needed to use his momentum.

I rotated my body out of his way, dodging his fist and kicking the back of his knee so he fell into the sand— I could tell he was surprised, but he recovered quickly. When he got up a second later, he managed to launch his fist into my cheekbone.

And, holy fuck, that hurt. It was like a burning heat across my face. When he drew his arm back to do it again, at least I was quick enough to block him. I felt like I could actually hear Drake telling me to keep my hands up.

I looked through the wall of water polo players and saw Drake trying to see over their heads. He actually was shouting advice.

Jordan was angry, which made for an erratic fighting style. I think he'd expected me to go down pretty easily and was pissed that I hadn't. Now he was fighting in front of an audience.

My knees were bent and my hands were up, so it was like I was standing in a modified warrior pose, and when

Jordan lunged forward again, I was in the perfect position to uppercut his chin.

Which I did, slamming Jordan into one of the giant blue coolers that Drake had unloaded from his car.

He got up quickly, and even though the fight hadn't been glamorous at all and I could still taste blood, I'd defended myself. Jordan had a bloody lip, and I was still on my feet.

And after I'd thrown him off me, I summoned whatever composure yoga had given me and promptly ignored it.

"You are pathetic, and Evey is out of your league," I said, spitting blood in the sand.

Jordan looked directly at Evey and said, "You were not worth it," before walking away with the rest of his friends.

"Let's go," said Evey, picking up our sweatshirts and putting her arm under mine to guide me to the car.

Drake and Jen followed us, and Drake was having a hard time not smiling.

"Are you okay?" Evey asked.

"I'm okay," I said.

"You're bleeding," she said.

"Like a warrior!" Drake shouted.

"Knock it off," said Jen, looking at him.

"That was awesome," he whispered.

Evey made sure I was buckled in and then started driving.

"I can't believe you got into a fight with Jordan. I'm so sorry."

"I'm not," I said.

"Why not?" she said.

"Because you are absolutely worth it," I told her.

Evey didn't say anything to that, but she held my hand while she drove me home.

"I'm sorry," she said.

"Don't be," I told her. "Maybe I'll have a scar now. That's hot, right?"

She squeezed my hand.

Namaste,
Leo

22

Today's Pose: Sphinx

Pretend you are a sphinx. End of pose.

Dear Journal,

Drake sent a text first thing in the morning.

> That was fucking awesome. I'll
> be there later to pick you up.

But no texts from Evey, which I thought was weird.
I even texted her.

> Hey you okay?

No response.

My dad hadn't been home last night, so I didn't have to explain my face to him until I woke up. And even then, it was a fairly quick explanation.

"Some guy wanted to fight me," I told him.

"Did you fight back?" Dad asked.

"Yeah," I said. He nodded in approval, and that was the extent of the conversation.

Later, when I threw my bag in Drake's car, he talked nonstop about the fight. About my stance. About the look I had in my eye. But I barely responded.

We got to the gym and I went straight to the desk.

Evey definitely looked like she'd been crying just now, and if there weren't a ton of people behind me waiting to sign in . . .

"Hey," I said.

"Later," she told me.

Well, I couldn't exactly ask her about it.

I don't have much else to say today, I guess.

I'll have to talk to her after class.

Today we're supposed to be doing handstands, and six months ago I never would have been able to do this. Now I'm pretty sure I'll be able to walk on my hands soon.

But I can't really concentrate because I keep thinking about Evey's face.

She was crying. She'd definitely been crying.

Namaste,
Leo

23

Dear Journal,

Evey wasn't there after class.

And she wasn't at work today. Some guy with a sweatband swiped my card. I tried texting her, but she didn't respond.

Drake told me why.

"I told Evey this was a bad idea. He's one of those guys who are always trying to impress somebody. He looks good on paper too. Good grades. Good test scores. And now an early acceptance to Duke and Brown." Then he said, "But it's worse than that. He's actually a bad guy, and Evey probably didn't know until it was too late because it's kinda a thing he and his friends do. Treat their girlfriends like princesses, then dump them, but not before embarrassing them.

It's creepy weird. Also, I once saw a dog outside back away from him when he walked by."

Drake leaned back as if this settled the matter.

"Okay, but that still doesn't tell me what made Evey cry," I said.

"He's got a photo, dude."

"A photo?"

"A photo of Evey."

"What kind of photo?" I didn't understand.

When I sat there looking particularly stupid, Drake put his hand on my shoulder and took a deep, patient breath. "The kind of photo you don't want anyone to see. The private kind."

It was like the wind had been knocked out of me completely.

I texted Evey.

Where are you? Can we talk?

And just waited for a reply.

Full handstand today, Journal. Held it for a full minute this time.

But that's really not what I want to talk about right now.

Namaste,
Leo

24

Today's Pose: Wild Thing

One poetic translation of Camatkarasana *is* "*the ecstatic unfolding of the enraptured heart.*"

But for me this pose is "*overturned turtle in need of assistance.*"

I can't even properly describe it. It's a little like bending your body into a bridge, then reaching one hand in the air behind you for something you can't see but you know is there.

Dear Journal,

I screwed up. I know I screwed up, but there's no way to make it better now. She won't even accept my apology. She's not responding to texts or phone calls.

There had been whispers at school. Drake said Jordan had circulated the photo to a few guys on his team.

I'd seen a few of them huddled over their phones laughing with twisted, completely evil faces. Because that's how it looks when you laugh at someone who is completely humiliated.

And I can't believe everything is unraveling now.

I could have said anything else to Evey.

I could have been supportive or kind or sympathetic.

I wasn't.

I'd met her at the gym after my last text.

"He took it while we were dating," she said.

And the first thing out of my mouth was: "Why would you take a picture like that?" I tried to take it back, but I'd already said it.

"I didn't know he was taking it," she said in a voice that sounded like someone small and breakable. Definitely not Evey.

I'll never forget that look on her face. The hurt. The confusion. The betrayal. It was like I'd exposed her all over again and I was part of the problem. And it was maybe five seconds before I realized the words had fallen out of my mouth, and I tried to take them back. When I reached out, she threw her arm back like I'd burned her.

"Don't touch me, Leo." She was already moving toward the door of the gym.

Jen had opinions on the subject too. When she saw me about half an hour later, she told me I was as bad as Jordan.

"Slut-shaming her when he's the creep. Nice, Leo. Nice."

Then Jen stormed off too.

And I don't want to come back here anymore. I don't think yoga is going to help after this. I don't know how I'll ever be able to think about anything else but that look on Evey's face.

Why would you take a picture like that?

Fuck yoga today.

25

Today's Pose: Child's Pose

Press your forehead into your mat with your knees bent. Flop arms out on either side of your body, keeping them close to your legs.

This is the pose you return to whenever you need a break but don't want to leave the room.

Sometimes it just feels good. Sometimes it is a silent cry for help.

Today it was a silent cry for help.

And I knew everyone would understand.

Dear Journal,

I don't feel well today.

I told everyone in class I'd be spending some time in child's pose, and I just never got up.

When I lifted my body after an hour, Annabelle and the rest of the class had formed a half circle around me with their mats. Like they were protecting me from the outside world.

It was weird. But I was in a mood to appreciate it.

Namaste,
Leo

26

Today's Pose: Pigeon

Naming a pose after a squat little bird is not a good idea.

But you start in a full push-up, then you place your left knee on the floor near your shoulder with left heel by right hip.

Then you lower yourself down over your leg and bend forward.

Then Annabelle says, "Pull navel in toward spine and tighten your pelvic-floor muscles."

I'm not sure how to do anything with my navel, and I'm not sure what my pelvic floor is.

Dear Journal,

I won't even pretend to write about yoga today. The rest of the class is writing something about the spiritual power we possess when we all work together to encourage each other, and I'm sitting here writing about the guy who has Evey's picture.

And I still want to vomit. I can taste the acid in my mouth.

What makes me feel the worst about this whole thing is not the picture itself. It's the moment before it was taken. The moment she believed she was safe, but wasn't. It kills me that this guy she trusted, maybe even cared about, saw her naked, and instead of thinking that that was a gift she'd bestowed on him, he used a photo to make her a joke.

No, not a joke. Something worse.

I take photos. I love them. I love the honesty. The finality. The emotion. Everything that you can do with a picture that you can't do with words. It all makes perfect sense to see someone and not have to say something about it. It has a language all its own, and that's why people say "A picture's worth a thousand words." Sometimes it's even better than a thousand words.

But sometimes it's worse.

Like those moments that could use a little explanation. A little understanding.

I told Drake she hates me and I don't think she'll ever speak to me again.

He shook his head and said, "She'll come around. She's upset. Well, more like furious and destroyed at the same time, and am I doing this right?" He was holding a ball of tangled yarn over one of the desks in Mr. Thomas's office.

Drake and I are still meeting with Mr. Thomas even

though it's clear we're not going to fight. Mr. Thomas looks pretty smug about that, actually. Like his little experiment with two troubled youths has paid off, and the Lifetime movie chronicling his success will be filmed very soon.

Drake was still using the time we spent in Mr. Thomas's office to learn to crochet.

His hands totally wanted to work faster, but the hook was small, and every time he stopped, he lost the rhythm of what he was doing. So I handed him a giant crochet hook and super-thick yarn, thinking it might be easier for him to work with. He had a whole granny square crocheted by the end of the hour.

The door to Mr. Thomas's office was open, and Sam, one of the guys on Drake's basketball team, walked by and did a double take at the two of us sitting there with huge balls of yarn, knitting needles, and crochet hooks. When the guy's face cracked into a wide smile and he looked like he was going to laugh, Drake said in a booming voice, "Motherfucker, keep walking, I am going to lose count on this pattern."

Mr. Thomas let the profanity slide.

I grinned, and Drake leaned back in his chair, shaking his head.

"Anyway, she doesn't hate you. Things just got really bad really quickly for her. And now everything is out of her control."

"Have other people actually seen the picture?" I asked, cringing.

"He says they have, and I wouldn't doubt it. Jordan is an asshole."

"Is there anything we can do at this point?" I asked him.

"You mean beat him up or something? Yeah, you totally could. That bonfire fight was just a warm-up."

"No, I didn't mean physical violence," I said.

"Oh, then, no," he said.

Namaste,
Leo

27

Today's Pose: Chair

Put your legs together and raise your arms high into the air as you bend your knees and imagine you are lowering yourself into a seated position.

Only don't do it. Do not lower yourself to the ground.

Just stay there in midair with your arms raised halfway between standing and sitting. The limbo of yoga poses.

Dear Journal,

I'm a week short of the hours I need to get my teacher training certification, but today is my last class.

Dad found out about ten minutes ago.

Drake tried to warn me that the self-defense class was sending out an email to all parents, inviting them to a demonstration. But I didn't get his texts before it happened. The demonstration was supposed to be earlier than class, so Dad left the house thinking I'd be there already.

I've never seen Dad so angry. He'd gone up to Drake's stepdad to introduce himself, and when the guy told Dad he'd never heard of me, that was it.

Dad opened and closed his fists, and the anger sort of flickered. The disappointment was so powerful he couldn't speak. It was literally choking him as I stood outside the yoga studio and faced him.

He looked at me, then turned around and left. So I just decided to come to this class anyway because I don't really have a reason not to. I could go home to a cloud of Greek anger, or I could do yoga one more time with my class.

So here I am.

Weird, I know.

Drake told me he stepped out of the demonstration when he saw my dad leave the room. He watched as Dad unsuccessfully demanded a refund, muttered something in Greek, and then went to stand outside the yoga studio door. Without blinking.

Drake asked if there was anything he could do to help, which is nice because I don't think I've ever had anyone ask me that question before. If they could help me somehow. But I think I just shook my head.

And I hope I said thank you, but I honestly can't remember.

Evey is still not here. She hasn't returned any of my texts, and she hasn't been to Greek school either.

Namaste,
Leo

Dear Mr. Ermou,

I'm the guy who punched Leo. The one who made you enroll him in that military fight training class. It's called military self-defense on the roster, but my stepdad, Brad, doesn't call it that because then it sounds like it's for women. Not sure why that matters, but it does to him, I guess.

I've been to your house several times, but I doubt Leo ever told you I was the one who punched him at school.

Anyway. Hi. How are you?

I know this is weird, but I wanted to say hi because Leo and I have actually become friends since this whole me-punching-him-in-the-face thing happened, and I think he's a good guy.

Which is weird coming from someone who hit him, but it's the truth.

I know he lied to you, which is messed up. But he's not just a weirdo who knits by himself and does secret yoga classes. I mean, he _is_ those things, but he's also a good person. And I'm pretty sure he lied to you because he felt like he couldn't be honest without you being disappointed.

I think, and stay with me here, I think he just feels everything. Like hard-core feels everything in his own Leo way. And that's not easy. I mean, I feel stuff sometimes and it sucks, so feeling stuff all the time must be heavy. It must make you tired.

I get that this is a weird letter to send, but I overheard you pulling Leo out of the yoga teacher training class. I heard you talking to the gym management and asking for a refund, and I guess I just wanted to say that as a guy who is now his friend, I really regret punching him.

He's also a good photographer.

His pictures are actually good. Not like fake good that you tell your friends when you don't want them to feel bad. For example, I have a friend who sings and thinks he's really good when actually he's a pretty shitty singer, so I have to lie. And I'm not a great liar so it might not matter, but at least I don't have to lie with Leo.

I think me telling you the truth about him being a good artist, maybe even a great one, might mean more coming from me. Since, you know, I once punched the guy in the face and I still like him.

He's also a really good knitter, which I know matters less to you, but he is. And he's teaching me. And speaking of teaching, I think it's a bad idea to take him out of teacher training, especially when he's so close to getting certified.

Then he could teach anywhere and someday get paid for it. And maybe you'd prefer that he was a translator like you or a lawyer or maybe in the military or something more dudes can get excited about, but you gotta know he hates that stuff.

So there it is. A stupid letter you probably won't read but that I had to send because Leo is my friend.

Sorry again for punching him.

I think we're cool now.

—Drake

28

Dear Journal,

Dad is still angry. It's like living with a ghost who slams doors.

But that's it. Just angry noises. Then nothing but silence as usual.

It's 4:00 a.m. Sleep has been unpredictable since I stopped doing yoga a week ago, because my mind is just running nonstop.

Insomnia is a problem. But I did finish two scarves, so at least it's been a productive problem. A few months ago, I'd been really used to doing everything alone, but now it's definitely not by choice. It's funny how fast alone can become lonely.

Dad has been working late somewhere in LA, translating some complicated documents for an elderly couple moving here from Glyfada. Drake is around but completely distracted by a looming math test that could jeopardize his place on the team.

And judging by Evey's angry silence and the looks she's given me at school, we won't be speaking anytime soon.

> Hey it's me. Can we talk? I'm sorry.

> Hey it's me again. I'm sorry.

> Sorry times infinity?

I sat on the floor of my Yia Yia's room going through my favorite prints. All of Evey's were lying in a neat stack. I spread them out and put them in chronological order. My eyes were immediately drawn to the one from the party where she kissed me the first time.

It doesn't feel right, writing this at a desk. It's weird not being in a gross, sweaty room with a bunch of other gross, sweaty people thanking each other for their glorious energy. It was weird, but I miss it. And I never thought I'd miss it.

Evey's Instagram post has gotten thousands of views.

The deadline for that photo contest is coming up, but it doesn't feel like something I want anymore. I mostly want to sleep, and I sit on the floor in Yia Yia's room and pretend everything is okay. But I heard my dad on the phone probably making plans for Greece, probably making good on his promise to send me to my cousins to toughen me up, and I don't even have it in me to talk him out of doing that.

I feel a little bit like I'm drowning inside my skin.

It's been a while since I visited Yia Yia. I think I'll visit this week so I can talk to her. Maybe if I'm lucky, she'll talk back. But actually, I hope not, because that would freak me out.

It's just that I used to talk to her whenever I felt like my head was overflowing with every anxious thought I've ever had. I've been thinking a lot about getting extra help. Like a prescription for something that might make me feel, I don't know, normal. No, not normal. Not sure that's possible. But better. Definitely better.

Yoga was helping, but it was never really enough on its own. And now it's not even an option.

So I guess this means I'll have to explain to Dad why I need a pill to feel okay.

I'm definitely not looking forward to that.

Maybe I'll take a sandwich and some snacks to the cemetery to eat with Yia Yia. Yeah, that'll definitely make it less weird.

Namaste,
Leo

P.S. I guess I don't need to end the entries with *namaste* if I'm not doing yoga right now. But it doesn't feel right without it.

Hey Evey. Have you heard from Leo today?

No.

He was supposed to meet me today for training.

Not my problem.

He's probably just late.

You know Leo is never late. And even if he were late, he wouldn't be this late.

How late is he?

2 hours

Try calling his dad.

I'm worried he's lying in a ditch somewhere. He's the kind of guy who thinks on time is late and early is on time.

I just texted Leo. No response.

His dad said he left his camera and his yarn bag at home.

29

Dear Journal,

I'm usually a pretty careful guy. I don't step too far away from my comfort zone, and I've never done anything that makes anybody worry.

Until yesterday.

I called the doctor Yia Yia took me to a few years back. I made an appointment to see her and we talked. About a lot of stuff.

Evey. Drake. Yoga.

Even yarn.

By the end of the session, she told me I had to come back and keep seeing her, and she wrote me a new prescription. But then she said the thing I didn't really want to deal with, though I knew it was coming.

"You need parental consent to fill this prescription."

I could go to therapy without telling Dad, but I needed his consent for the medication. And this time Yia Yia wasn't around to talk him into it. But I had to ask anyway. Even if the answer was no.

Dad was sitting in his chair, looking down at his phone, when I dropped the form in his lap. I took a deep breath while he read it, and braced myself, thinking I'd have to explain why I need help.

Turns out I didn't have to explain anything.

He looked up at me and asked, "You need this?"

I nodded, and he signed it, and when he looked at me, it was a different expression than I remember. Not pride, but definitely not embarrassment.

I thought maybe he just didn't want to talk about it. A lot of his decisions are made in an effort to avoid conversation, but then he said, "I hope this helps."

And I didn't know how the fuck to respond to that, so I said thanks and got the hell out.

I went straight to the pharmacy and then went to visit Yia Yia.

After I took a couple of those pills, I felt calm and happy and completely at peace. And I'd just eaten lunch, so I was also full. And it was the best feeling.

I found myself wondering what the hell I'd been waiting for. I mean, what had stopped me from taking this stuff when my brain was turning into a tiny clapping monkey juggling knives on a tightrope?

But I ignored the doc's warning that I should try the new medication at home to see how it might affect me.

So anyway I fell asleep. For four hours.

For a stone bench in a cemetery, it was actually a pretty comfortable nap.

Apparently, during that time Drake was worried and went back to the gym to look for me. When I wasn't there, he tried calling Evey.

A shit ton of texts later, they got desperate and called Dad. Since I was usually at school, home, or the gym, and I was at none of those places.

It was Dad who realized right away where I might be.

So when I opened my eyes at the cemetery he was sitting right next to me on the bench.

"Hi," I said.

"Hi," he said back.

He looked tired.

"I don't remember the last time I was here," he said, looking around.

"The funeral?" I suggested, sitting up.

"Maybe," he said.

"I come here a lot."

"I know," said Dad, leaning his elbows on his knees and holding his chin in his hands.

"How?" I asked. I never got the impression that he cared where I was, but he held out his phone and there was a little dot marked LEO.

"You tracked me?" I asked, impressed and a little horrified.

"Someone at the phone store showed me how to use it. I don't do it all the time. Just have it for emergencies."

"You could have just asked," I said. He bowed his head a little.

"We're not doing so well. Our little family. Are we?" he asked.

"I don't know," I said.

Then there was silence and it was familiar because Dad was there.

After a while he broke it.

"Why did you stop taking the self-defense class?" he asked.

"I never took it," I told him. "There were huge guys in there beating the shit out of each other. And I didn't want to disappoint you again. So I took yoga."

"And you liked it?"

"No, I hated it. At first. But now, yeah. I like it."

Dad nodded.

"I'm sorry I lied to you."

"Let's go home," he said.

"You know that prescription you signed off on? One of the common side effects is sleepiness, so that's why I passed out." I looked at him and then immediately looked down at the ground.

He was quiet for a minute. Then he said, "On Wednesday nights, I've been seeing a grief therapist."

I stared at him.

"I never did anything after your mother died. And then

after Yia Yia, it all sort of just came up again. So I've been seeing someone."

"I thought you were working late."

"I know you did. I wanted you to think that," he said. "I'm sorry I lied to you too."

"Can we go home now?" I asked.

We walked to the car not saying anything, but it didn't feel forced or weird now. It felt like something had opened, and I imagined Yia Yia sitting there through the whole conversation.

● ● ●

Evey was waiting in the driveway when we got home. Dad had texted her (and Drake too) to say I was okay, and I guess I just underestimated how pissed Evey would be.

Her eyes were the first thing I noticed.

Dark, angry, but just a tiny bit relieved. "You absolute fucking idiot."

Dad walked directly inside, leaving me outside with Evey. "How could you just be lying there asleep with a bunch of dead people? No note, no message to anyone who might care where you are. You're just lying there. What the fuck is your problem?"

She was yelling a lot, and usually yelling is one of those trigger things that pushes the adrenaline and makes my body think it's supposed to be running from a bear, but there was something nice about it. There was genuine concern. That's

225

why it was nice, I thought. And I wasn't anxious. I was still sleepy from the pill I took. She was still yelling at me when I interrupted her.

"Evey?"

"What?" Her eyes were devoid of any warmth because she was throwing so much anger from them. Like tiny laser beams.

But I knew that was my chance.

"I'm sorry," I said. "I'm sorry about what I said about the picture. It doesn't matter how he got it. Or if you gave it to him. It just matters that he's a creep for using it."

Evey was quiet for a minute.

I wanted to laugh because she wanted to still be mad at me.

"Actually I think it *does* matter how he got it," she said. "He took it with the camera on his computer, without my permission, without me knowing. And now he's planning to send it everywhere."

"Am I forgiven?" I asked stupidly. I'm pretty sure I slurred a little as she sat me down on the bench by the front door.

She looked for a second like she wanted to say no. Then her expression changed as she leaned forward and kissed me. Quickly, softly. Then she wrapped her arms around me and rested her cheek on my chest.

"I started to not mind being blackmailed," I said. "And it didn't matter to me that Yia Yia said your family was bad luck."

She laughed.

We were quiet for a long time until she let her fears surface again.

"He has the picture. And he's angry. There's nothing I can do."

"Well, not nothing," I said.

She raised an eyebrow.

"How often do you think he changes the passcode for his phone?"

Namaste,
Leo

30

Dear Journal,

You know how you can know that someone loves you but doesn't like you very much? That's how I've always felt about my dad. I know he wouldn't take care of me, provide for me, or do any of the stuff that dads normally do if he didn't love me, but I couldn't really say with certainty that he likes me.

But the love part is what matters even if everything else is off.

When Evey went home, my dad was standing in the doorway, looking at me like he'd never really seen me before.

I remember telling him again that I was sorry and then I remember him kissing the top of my head and telling me to go to bed. We both sort of stared at each other after that. That hadn't happened in recent memory, and I couldn't wrap my head around it. Then he turned to me again and said, "If you like it, go back to yoga."

Jesus, it had been a weird day.

So namaste, I guess?
Leo

31

Dear Journal,

Two days later Drake, Jen, and Evey were at my house before I woke up.

Drake is abrupt under regular circumstances, but hearing him walk down my hallway before I'd even gotten out of bed to pee was a new level.

He put some weird kale fruit smoothie on my nightstand and turned back to the door while Jen and Evey stepped in holding coffees.

"So Leo would have to distract Jordan, and I would have to steal the phone?" Drake said.

"Exactly. And Jen and I will watch the door while you're doing it," Evey said.

"Don't people ever leave the room during hot yoga? What if someone comes in? How would we stop them?" Jen said, throwing my backpack unceremoniously on the floor so she could sit in my desk chair.

Then they all turned to me.

"Hi?" I said.

"Dude," said Drake, wrinkling his nose. "Your breath."

"Bite me," I said.

Evey sat down on the edge of my bed, holding her coffee. I was suddenly aware of how I look in the morning. And how much dirty laundry was lying on my floor. I would have tried to say something funny to distract from the moment, but Drake picked up a knitting magazine with a smiling old lady petting an alpaca and held it up, pointing and shaking his head.

"So," Evey said. "We've been discussing ways to steal Jordan's phone, and I think we've decided that you'll need to take a yoga class with him."

I did a confused-puppy head tilt.

"You take class with Jordan. Make sure he doesn't leave the room. I steal phone. Evey and Jen cover me," Drake said slowly like Tarzan. Jen nodded, examining some of the fluffier balls of yarn on my desk.

"Do you think you can handle taking a yoga class with a bunch of jocks? One of whom you recently punched in the face?" Jen looked at me serenely, and I felt like I was missing something. I sat up to face Evey.

"How are you going to get a bunch of athletes to

voluntarily take a hot yoga class?" I asked her, but before Evey could answer, Jen laughed.

"Oh," she said. "That's the genius part. By turning it into a competition."

Evey handed me a flyer she'd folded into her bag. It was emblazoned with:

CAN YOU HANDLE THE HEAT?

It was a competition with a five-dollar entry fee. All proceeds would go to the California Women's Foundation. And the team that signed up the most people for the hot yoga class would win the grand prize: free transportation to prom with their choice of stretch Hummer, stretch Suburban, or Oscar Mayer Wienermobile.

"The Wienermobile?" Drake laughed. "How?"

"My parents know the owners of the limo company," Evey said blandly, staring at the flyer.

"Evey, this competition is Friday," I said.

"Yes, it is," she said, smiling.

"How are you going to get anyone to participate? It's not enough time."

"She put this into motion days ago," Jen said. "She's already contacted all the team coaches, and they've already committed all their athletes to go out there and get people signed up."

"Water polo is already on board," Drake added. He was still flipping through the knitting magazine.

"Okay, but even if we do this, and even if we steal the phone, there's a chance this won't matter," I said. And I felt bad the minute I'd said it, because I was the one who originally made the suggestion.

But then Drake was the one who went deep: "We have to *try* even if it doesn't work. Trying to protect someone matters too."

• • •

I assumed I was going to have to ask Drake for a ride, but then Dad got up to take me to class, and I just told Drake to let him. Dad even talked to me in the car. Well, actually, he kinda just talked AT me, but it was definitely an enormous effort to communicate. Then, when he dropped me off, it was with a weird wave, and he almost raised his hand to do a high five. He was trying, so I let it slide.

• • •

And now the day has arrived.

Evey managed to quietly publicize the competition to the point that the gym had to open all its rooms for the day and bring in more teachers to accommodate the crowd of people who had signed up. Eventually the gym had to start turning people away. But the crazy thing was that people still wanted to donate so their team could win.

Jen, Drake, and I were waiting in the self-defense room

before the whole thing was supposed to start, and Evey came in looking panicked.

"The water polo team is going to bail," she said. "Jordan told Annabelle that he and his team all walk unless they get some kind of 'designation' for raising the most money. Like some kind of extra prize that sets them apart from other people."

"Designation?" said Drake. "Because transportation to prom isn't enough? That slimy bastard."

"I don't know what we can give them," Evey said, and she looked like she was actually starting to sweat. "All the yoga shirts in the lobby are ridiculously expensive, and we didn't have any cheap shirts made, so . . ."

"Give them the headbands," I said, remembering the basket on the check-in desk. "There are more in the back."

Evey's eyes lit up, and she was about to turn to race out the door.

"Wait," I said. "Drake and I will get them."

Evey looked confused, and Drake raised an eyebrow but didn't say anything as we hurried to the supply room, dodging crowds of people. I pulled down the box of blue headbands I'd made to sell. And found the one black-and-blue headband at the bottom.

"A captain's headband," I said.

Then I turned to the staff bathroom, whose door was slightly ajar, and dropped the headband into the toilet bowl with a splash.

"Dude . . . ," Drake said in what was clearly a proud and encouraging tone. "How are you gonna dry it?"

I grabbed the plunger on the floor and used it to lift the headband out of the water before hitting the air dryer with my elbow and dangling the headband underneath to dry it. Then I wrapped it in the tissue paper that had been stuffed in the box, and we walked back out to the front.

"Here," I told Annabelle. "This box is for the winning water polo team. Tell them these are handmade, one hundred percent cotton. And this," I said, holding the tissue-wrapped headband, "is for their captain, Jordan. The guy who said they were going to bail. Can you give it to him?"

Annabelle smiled and raced the box over to the team, who cheered. And when Jordan unwrapped his headband from the tissue and placed it on his head like a crown, the rest of the team cheered again.

"Dude," said Drake. "That's fucking beautiful."

And thinking about the dirty shit toilet water that would be mixing with his sweat and dripping down his face pretty soon, I couldn't help but agree.

We ran back to the staff room, and Drake gave Evey the thumbs-up.

"And you still know his passcode, right?" I asked.

She looked at me patiently.

"Okay then."

The whole water polo team walked into the yoga room, and now we wait.

The minute class starts, the men's locker room will be empty, meaning Evey can grab Jordan's phone. Yoga classes always start on time, and you're not allowed out of the room or into the room once class has started.

Hello, anxiety, my old friend.

I suppose I should spend a second addressing how unnerving this is thus far. I mean, I've trained myself to feel completely at ease in yoga, to let the world outside vanish as I worship at the altar of stretchy pants, weird toe socks, and the random fart we all pretend to ignore.

But now they're all talking, and I can hear Jordan's voice. He's laughing about something, and I try to imagine Evey waiting for class to begin so she can come out of hiding.

She and Drake are both waiting for their opening to run into the men's locker room, grab his phone, and delete the picture she knows he's holding on to.

And it might not matter. It might even make things worse. But we have to try.

Because Drake is right. Trying to protect someone matters too.

Deep breaths.

Namaste,
Leo

Evey,

    That was a pretty impressive stunt, even for you.

    Did you really think you could destroy the evidence by deleting a photo from my phone? I didn't realize you were that stupid.

    Photos are everywhere. Every time someone takes a picture it lives forever. Plus, I have it saved other places, and other people have seen it.

    And more people will see it soon, because I don't think you fully understand what you've done.

    Were you honestly trying to get me in trouble with my parents? Do you even think they'd understand your weird photo shoot and all the "hidden" messages in it?

    And the shitty part for you is that none of it matters.

    You're pathetic. And if you think your little photo shoot is going to be anything but a bitter ex-girlfriend trying to get even with some guy for breaking up with her, you're a bigger loser than I thought.

    Thanks for the laugh, though.

    Stay tuned for some interesting posts on my Instagram account, leading my followers to a great little site that houses photos like that.

    There's no hiding now.

    Everyone will know you're a slut.

                               –J

32

Dear Journal,

Evey came over to my house after she got the letter from
Jordan. She showed it to me, and neither of us said anything
for a long time. We just sat in my room on my bed staring
at it, both of us probably willing the letters to change into
something else.

It's impossible to know what could have been going on
in her head, and she isn't the type to share every single emotion inside her, so we sat there in silence and let the gravity
of this fucking awful mess swallow us whole.

It's hard to be a person with feelings sometimes. It's hard
to absorb all of the stress and pain of other people around
you and keep it under control. It's especially hard to pretend

that something doesn't bother me, because I've never learned how to do that properly. I've never learned how to show the face I want everyone else to see.

So I cried.

First it was just silent tears that I wiped away as quick as I could when I felt them burning at the corners of my eyes, and then it was the heavy downpour that I just let fall down my face without acknowledging its existence. If I pretended like I wasn't crying, no one would know. It was a genius plan.

But Evey looked at me, and instead of wiping my tears away or saying anything at all, she found a spot just under my arm and leaned into it, resting her head against my shoulder. She wasn't crying, but her mouth was in a thin line and she was looking ahead like the force of her thoughts could blast a hole in the wall.

I stopped crying and my breathing slowed and I think it's the most comfortable I've ever been in my entire life, sitting on that bed, just absorbing a terrible feeling. Not talking. Not trying to figure anything out. Just letting the awfulness pour down on top of us.

"Well, we did everything," she said finally, and I looked at her with teary eyes, and she actually laughed.

"You'd think someone had a naked photo of *you*," she said, burrowing deeper into my chest.

I leaned back against the wall and breathed into her hair.

"I'm sorry this happened," I said.

She looked at me.

"I'm not," she said.

"How can you say that? I mean, not to freak you out or make this any worse, but he wins. He has everything, and there's nothing we can do to stop him."

"You should be a motivational speaker," she said calmly.

And that's the weird part. She said it *calmly*. Like nothing terrible was happening, and there wasn't anything to be worried about. My intestines were tangling themselves into tiny little knots, and I could already feel my lungs working harder for oxygen.

"You know I'm right," I said.

"Probably," she said. Then she squeezed my hand, and I felt like I might have been missing something because she still looked calm.

Is this how people handle their shit if they don't have anxiety?

Bad stuff happens and you just deal with it? You don't ramp up every emotion you have ever experienced or replay every situation until you've convinced yourself that there is some way to go back in time and undo the past?

"Just breathe, Leo," she said.

So I did.

Namaste,
Leo

Dear Ms. Paros,

I must admit, your article proposal was definitely unorthodox, which is why it was originally rejected.

But as luck would have it, I was just promoted to senior editor and had the opportunity to look through a few older submissions we passed on in previous issues. In the spirit of sisterhood (and because I loved your pitch), HuffPost would like to publish your article "Revenge and Bad Luck."

As for the photographs, let's set up a call to discuss. When are you available?

Elle Tabshouri
Senior Editor
HuffPost

33

Dear Journal,

The article ran a week ago. And it was fucking brilliant.

I read every word. Then I read it again and again. Then I brought it to the cemetery and read it to Yia Yia, which is really absurd when you think about it, because you should be able to talk to dead people anywhere. But maybe there's just something comforting about being able to go somewhere to miss someone and feel close to them again.

Evey hadn't told me her pitch had been accepted or that she'd even sent it. I think she wanted to surprise me with it. And that surprise was actually worth the extra anxiety it caused afterward.

Usually, big publications don't work like that. They don't include an article from a new writer in a huge publication like that, and they certainly don't run the article only a few days after accepting it, but the planets seemed to align in Evey's favor to make this work. Even the editor who read the article said it was not a regular thing.

Then she went on to say that she really liked Evey's style and that she'd be open to reading other stuff from her in the future. Which is, like, insane. After getting nothing but rejections, to get a positive response was incredible. But with a price, of course. There's always a price for good stuff.

Because there was a certain degree of awful still to contend with. Evey had to have a conversation with her parents beforehand because she was basically revealing herself before someone else got a chance to. On her own terms. Not with the picture itself, obviously, but with the actual story, and she said they seemed to understand. Her dad didn't really want to look at her for a while, but she says he'll get over it eventually. I don't think anyone wants to think of their child in that way, but I think they like the idea of her being used even less.

Anyway, the article was perfect. It didn't tiptoe around the fact that this creep was trying to make Evey out to be the bad guy. The one who was asking for it by putting herself in a vulnerable position.

But thinking about other people and the influence they might have got me thinking about Jordan and his parents. Of course Evey would have met them. She would have spent a considerable amount of time at his house, around his family, so it made perfect sense that she'd know them.

And she knew HuffPost bulletins and news articles always popped up on his mom's phone and that she was a sucker for breakup stories and celebrity gossip. Jordan used to tease her about it. So the title "Revenge and Bad Luck" was enough to draw her in.

Evey wrote it well. She described the pictures, the yarn, and even the part I didn't want to read: the moments leading up to the photo he took without her knowing. Those moments of complete vulnerability with someone she trusted.

I memorized my favorite lines:

> It wasn't easy for me to admit that I was wrong about someone. I didn't want him to be that guy who used me, because then it meant I was the girl who was used. And to make matters worse—I trusted him, and he didn't deserve it.
>
> And even though I've always wanted to write for magazines, I never expected that the first story I published would be so revealing or that the first publication that I published with would be so crucial. Because his mom reads HuffPost quite a bit.
>
> So, Vivian, if you're reading this: Your son still has the picture. And has others of other girls.
>
> Please don't let him send them.

It was a genius move and also the bravest thing she's ever done, because he could still post the photos to a revenge porn site at any time. Even though Evey is underage. He could have someone else post it to multiple sites. He could still do something horrible.

"But at least his parents will know what a complete douchebag he is," I told her.

"No," she said. "The point is that *everyone* will know what a complete douchebag he is. And if I'm not afraid to admit that the photo exists, then it doesn't have nearly the power he thinks it does."

She was right. It was about power. More importantly, it was about surrendering power. Something Evey would never voluntarily do.

Then she leaned in to me and wanted to know if the photography contest had responded.

We'd tagged the contest organizers in the photos, and I'd finally updated my account with new photos and contact information, so everything had been submitted.

All of the yarn-bombing shots were there, but there was one more thing I wanted to include that didn't have much to do with the revenge theme—still, luck was important to both of us.

I crocheted a few matis in various sizes, and I took a photo of the moment I handed them out.

Evey's smirk as I handed her a tiny one about the size of a quarter and she held it in the palm of her hand.

Drake's raised eyebrow as he held up a mati the size of a basketball and then tossed it like a pizza.

My dad's blank expression as he lifted it up and held it out over his chest where his heart should be. All of them holding the matis I made and reacting to me telling them that I was wishing them good luck.

"Sorry, but you're still probably cursed, Leo." Evey grinned.

"So, about that," I said, pulling out a small wrapped package from my bag. "Obviously, I can't find the one he stole to give back to you. But I thought . . ." I trailed off as she opened the box.

Inside was an icon like the one Stavros had stolen. It was an image of Mary cradling the baby Jesus with a black-and-burgundy background.

"Did you make this?" Evey asked, raising an eyebrow.

"Cross-stitch. And gold embroidery," I said.

"It probably isn't exactly like the one he stole, but maybe it'll work." She smiled.

"So do the thing," I said.

"What thing?" she asked.

"The thing where you officially release my family from the curse."

"I officially release you and your family from the curse, Leo."

I looked around. Nothing happened.

"Maybe you said it wrong," I mused.

• • •

Those were the last photos in the submission, and even if I don't win, some other pretty great stuff happened as a result of Evey's article and Instagram posts.

I got, like, six thousand followers overnight. Tons of people wanted me to take their photo. And then, the coolest part—which probably means nothing, but: the Rhode Island School of Design liked my contest submission.

I know that's not a huge deal. Plenty of strangers can like your post if you leave it public, but someone at my dream school saw it. Someone at my dream school liked the photos and thought they were worth something. Worth liking, at least.

I was getting a lot of messages from people who had seen the photos and liked my work.

Okay, so I might be getting carried away, but that's a cool ego boost.

And I actually had a hard time sleeping after the post got so much attention. Sucks that even good stuff causes a bad reaction in my brain. Calm is still hard to hold on to, and I decided to delete a bunch of apps from my phone because the constant notifications were hard to process all day long.

And my Etsy sales almost crashed the site.

Okay, not really, but there were a ton of orders. I had to close it temporarily.

And I've already sold about thirty yoga headbands because they're so easy to make. The gym still lets me sell them in a basket by the front desk with a little sign. It's a small thing, but it actually does feel good to sell stuff I make. Drake has five headbands in assorted colors.

Then I overheard my dad telling my aunt in Greece all

about it. He said that my sales were good and that my photography was really taking off.

He doesn't say I "dabble" in photography anymore.

Namaste,
Leo

34

Today's Pose: Warrior

You start this pose with your legs apart. Bring hands to your hips. Relax the shoulders. Extend your arms. Face your palms down.

Bend your knee, keeping knee over ankle. Gaze out over right hand like a king casually observing his troops.

Dear Journal,

Today I am a yogi.

I have completed my training and I can teach my first official class. So I got to invite everyone.

Including Evey and Drake, who protested but came

anyway. The room was filling up, and everyone was laying out the mats and getting their water bottles filled. It was even starting to feel like a regular class until I remembered that I'd need to be standing in the front of the room guiding everyone through the poses.

And I couldn't figure out if I was keeping this up and getting this certification because I'd already committed so much time to it or if it was because it actually felt good to do yoga. Both, I guess.

Drake introduced himself to everyone sitting around him, and instead of overwhelming them with a barrage of verbal diarrhea, he was acting like an honest-to-God normal guy. And he was almost—

"Charming?" he suggested when I searched for the right word.

"I wouldn't go that far," I said.

"Leo, I am a stud muffin whose hotness cannot be contained." He then unzipped his hoodie to reveal a pink tank top. He seemed different than he usually does. He just told me that his doctor had finally prescribed something that was helping with his focus issues.

Amazing what can happen when a doctor listens.

And when Drake asked me if I was taking anything, I said, "Yep. It's helping, and I don't know why I ever stopped."

And I was pretty convinced that my dad was still embarrassed about the whole yoga thing. That he somehow thought I was still bringing shame to our family by sweating on a mat in front of strangers in stretchy pants.

Then he showed up thirty seconds ago.

He's got a mat under his arm and a Fiji Water bottle in his hand and he looks more lost than he's ever been in his life, but he's standing in the middle of this room full of strangers because I asked him to be here. I just never in a million years thought he'd come.

And no, it's not like he walked over and said, *I'm proud of you, son. I'm sorry I doubted you.* But he's here. He got the invitation that I shoved under his door when I left this morning, and he showed up. I'll take that. Then he also pulls out of his pocket one of the headbands I crocheted and looks at the logo I stitched on. A crocheted mati inside a camera lens. He puts it on his head and gives me a thumbs-up.

I've never seen him do a thumbs-up before, and I want to laugh, but I just smile because I can't believe he's here.

The clock says I still have five minutes, so I'm waiting for stragglers and trying to calmly finish this entry, but I can't stop staring at my dad. He's wearing cotton pants and a white T-shirt that he's already sweating through. He just opened his water bottle and drank half of it. Now he's trying to find a way to get comfortable. It looks like hard work. He's just standing there now, trying to be calm. Trying to figure out what comes next.

He's talking with his eyes. And they're saying: *This is weird and I very much don't want to be here right now, but I am and I'm not leaving.*

We might not be much closer to understanding each other, but at least the door is open.

There's probably never going to be a lot of conversation. He isn't the type to talk about stuff for hours. But he does stuff now. He's making an effort. Like, he signed us up for a Greek cooking class together, which is a lot of togetherness, but I guess it's necessary because our food situation has gotten pretty terrible. And if I go, I can at least do half the cooking. That's probably what he's thinking.

"A class with other people?" I asked when he told me.

"Yes. Sorry," he said.

Then we both laughed and it wasn't even funny. The cooking teacher, as it turns out, is a pretty woman named Voula, so maybe it wasn't such a selfless act.

We decided to clear out Yia Yia's room instead of keeping it as a creepy shrine, and, honestly, I think she'd be okay with that. My dad even said I could have it, so I'm converting it into a studio. One side filled with cubbyholes for yarn and one side with a huge white desk and two giant dual monitors for touching up digital photos. There's even space in the middle for me to do yoga if I want to practice at home because who knows if I'll ever teach it anywhere? Who'd have even thought that would be a consideration?

I wondered what Yia Yia would have thought of this. How she would have felt about the way everything had worked out.

Proud, agapi mou. That's what she would have said.

I need to remind myself to breathe. To spend more time breathing out than in. And I need to remember that yoga is medicine too.

Then Evey walks up to me and I smile. A real smile. Because the photo contest mailed me an envelope. A big one. I haven't opened it yet, but if the same rule for college letters applies, then a big, thick envelope is good news, right?

She raises herself up and kisses me, and when I open my eyes again, the rest of the room is laughing, but not in a mean way.

Then she wishes me luck and walks over to a mat in the back of the room, where Jen is waiting for her.

She wished me luck in Greek.

And she called me Leonidas.

Namaste,
Leo

35

Dear Journal,

It's summer. Which means no school and no mandated sessions with Mr. Thomas, but, true to form, Drake still sends me motivational texts every day.

> Drop that gas station burrito, you animal.

> Punch like you knit. WITH DETAIL AND PRECISION. START WITH A QUALITY ATTITUDE. SAME WAY YOU'D START WITH QUALITY FIBERS.

> You are a magnificent beast.

He's even more over the top than usual because he managed to squeak by in math without having to do summer school so now he feels like heaven has handed him his freedom.

I usually roll my eyes at his texts, but who'd have thought I'd actually appreciate the encouragement? And who'd have thought I'd learn to enjoy human interaction?

I mean, not parties or anything. Don't be ridiculous. But having people in my life.

And I usually receive these gems on Wednesdays, when I now teach a beginners' yoga class at the gym.

For something that happened completely by luck, I'm really happy with how everything turned out. Yoga plus mild anxiety medication plus healthier outlook on social experiences has helped tremendously. And Mr. Thomas, I guess.

If he hadn't forced me and Drake to hang out in a room together, breathing the same air and staring at the same stupid poster of Mister Rogers telling us to believe in ourselves or some crap, we never would have talked. And we never would have become friends.

I thought about knitting Mr. Thomas something as a thank-you, but guess what. Drake already did it.

He knit him a mati.

The weirdest, most crooked, oval-shaped mati I've ever seen, but the luck is probably still good. Even if Drake did it.

And Drake told him he could pin it to his bulletin board with all the other crappy art that kids give him.

My therapist has a board like that too. Covered in crappy art.

Oh yeah, I have a therapist. Like, a regular one who I visit and talk to like a grown-up. It seemed like the smart thing to do, given that I'd like to keep feeling okay.

And this is how I do that. This is how I take care of myself.

I don't always know how I'm doing until someone asks me about it, so talking about feelings is kind of my thing now.

Because while I'm seeing my own therapist for anxiety, Dad also invited me to talk to his therapist about grief.

And it was uncomfortable.

Like, really uncomfortable.

Like the emotional equivalent of bees in your underwear uncomfortable because I can't remember ever seeing my dad cry. Not when Mom died. Not when Yia Yia died. NEVER.

I think all of that emotional constipation or whatever it was finally caught up with him to the point that it looked like he was giving birth to some very hard feelings.

But we survived it, and we talked. Mostly about how we can include each other in our lives. The counselor says the goal is to eventually talk about stuff we're worried about, and in my head, I was like: *Wait, I have to come back?*

But I think it'll be good for us.

We're already doing better. Our fridge even looks like real people live in our house.

Anyway, at the end of the session she asked us if there were any thoughts we'd like to end on, and my dad goes, "If your girlfriend is coming over and you need privacy, please let me know. I don't want to walk in on anything."

I laughed.

He laughed.

And we went home to make stuffed tomatoes from Yia Yia's recipe.

Drake and Evey and Jen are all coming over to see how we do with it.

If we screw it up, Yia Yia is definitely going to haunt us.

Namaste,
Leonidas

Author's Note

Dear Reader,

Leo's experience with Greekness, yoga, yarn work, and anxiety are based on my own experience.

I'm Greek on my dad's side. I practice yoga. I crochet. And I've had anxiety for most of my life.

The insomnia and difficulty falling asleep, the weird stomach clenching, the jittery panicked feeling that makes you hot and sweaty all over when you feel like you're losing control . . . all mine.

As a kid, I didn't know how to handle the anxiety. As an adult, I still find it challenging to manage at times.

I guess I'd like to tell you that I was the kid who cried at school and I am the adult who still struggles with keeping my head above that rising feeling of panic.

It is more than okay to talk to a professional about anxiety.

It is more than okay to get medication for anxiety.

It is even okay to have anxiety.

In fact, learning how to manage my anxiety is probably what drew me to writing. It was another way for me to regain control by creating worlds of my own. So it's hard to hate my anxiety completely, even though some days I do.

Just find what works for you, and go for it. Don't let anyone make you feel small for taking care of your mental health.

One more thing: Leo acknowledges his anxiety but not the underlying trauma that caused it. He does not yet have that level of understanding of his own mental health, because many doctors do not assess for traumatic events when diagnosing anxiety. So while Leo *is* dealing with his anxiety, it is also important not to minimize the initial trauma that set everything in motion (his mother's death).

However, since the story ends with a positive experience with medication and therapy, I firmly believe that Leo will discuss these concepts with his therapist in more depth in the future.

With love,

Julia

Acknowledgments

I have a lot of people to thank for helping me on this journey:

My editor, Chelsea Eberly, who midwifed this book. It was a hard labor, but eventually the story was born because she believed in it and because she believed in me. I'm so grateful for her hard work and that of the whole team at Random House, including the phenomenal work of copy-editors Barbara Bakowski and Barbara Perris and the artistic talents of art director Angela Carlino and designers Philip Pascuzzo and Larsson McSwain.

On that note, I'd also like to add a special thank-you to Polo Orozco for carrying this book over the finish line! Polo, you are awesome!

Thanks to my previous agent, Heather Flaherty, who started it all. Words cannot possibly express how much your faith meant to me when I was in the query trenches, and how much it still means to me now.

A HUGE thank-you to my current agent, Jodi Reamer. Looking forward to all the stories to come!

My parents and in-laws, who continue to amaze me with their love and support.

EVERY SINGLE PERSON I SWINDLED INTO BABYSITTING MY CHILDREN SO I COULD GET SOME WRITING DONE: my sisters, Cassandra and Athena; my friends Kortney Hughes and Lauren Davis. And of course the real MVPs, my mom, Linda, and mother-in-law, Margaret. *ROUND OF APPLAUSE* My babies are my world, but they're also awake A LOT, so having the extra backup is important. It really does take a village.

Dr. Liana Georgoulis, who patiently answered all my anxiety-related questions and helped me develop Leo's character with more depth and sensitivity.

All the instructors at Core Power Yoga, who guided my feet and introduced me to yoga when I needed it most.

Ming Loong Teo, LCSW, whose professional experience and commentary brought more clarity to Leo's diagnosis and to the overall discussion of mental health.

My students at Orange County School of the Arts, who blessed me with their enthusiasm and made every class an adventure. I LOVE YOU ALL!

My husband, Doug, and my children Alexandria, Charlotte, and James, who fill my life with beauty and chaos. Every day with you is a gift. I love you so much.

Kiria Isa, my Boulia, who always made me feel important and told me all the stories I wasn't supposed to hear. I wish I could take her to see my books in the wild so she could tell strangers that I'm a published writer. But, to be honest, she is probably haunting bookstores now and shoving my work in people's hands anyway.

About the Author

JULIA WALTON is the author of the award-winning *Words on Bathroom Walls*. She received an MFA in creative writing from Chapman University and a BA in history from the University of California, Irvine. Julia lives with her husband and children in Huntington Beach, California.

JULIAWALTON.COM